BT95
22

11-99

	DATE DUE	

For Sarah
For Everything,
For Always

What
She
Left
Me

The
Katharine Bakeless Nason
Literary Publication Prizes

The Bakeless Literary Publication Prizes are sponsored by the Bread Loaf Writers' Conference of Middlebury College to support the publication of first books. The manuscripts are selected through an open competition and are published by University Press of New England/Middlebury College Press.

Competition Winners in Fiction

1996
Katherine L. Hester, *Eggs for Young America*
judge: Francine Prose

1997
Joyce Hinnefeld, *Tell Me Everything and Other Stories*
judge: Joanna Scott

1998
Judy Doenges, *What She Left Me*
judge: Richard Bausch

What She Left Me

Stories
and a
Novella

JUDY DOENGES

MIDDLEBURY COLLEGE PRESS
Published by University Press of New England
Hanover and London

Middlebury College Press

Published by University Press of New England, Hanover, NH 03755

© 1999 by Judy Doenges

All rights reserved

Printed in the United States of America 5 4 3 2

CIP data appear at the end of the book

The author wishes to acknowledge the publication of several of the stories in this collection, some in slightly different form, in the following: *The Georgia Review*, "What She Left Me"; *Our Mothers/Our Selves*, "What She Left Me"; *Equinox*, "MIB"; *Nimrod*, "Crooks"; *Phoebe*, "The Money Stays, The People Go"; *The Chattahoochee Review*, "Occidental"; *Ohio Short Fiction*, "Disaster"; *Green Mountains Review*, "The Whole Numbers of Families"; *Permafrost*, "Incognito"; *Evergreen Chronicles*, "God of Gods."

The author wishes to thank Artist Trust and the Ragdale Foundation for support during the writing of some of this work.

Contents

What
She
Left
Me

What
She
Left
Me

A COMPLETE SET OF BARWARE. Including: twelve each of high-ball, old-fashioned, martini, and mint julep glasses (for the Derby, brought out once a year); sixty champagne flutes bought for an anniversary party canceled because of divorce; fifty etched wineglasses, sets of cordial glasses, brandy snifters, aperitif glasses, mugs for toddies, sixteen cut glass water tumblers (all chipped); swizzle sticks from (among other places) The Palmer House, the Pump Room, Cape Cod Room, and the Bali-Hai in Arlington Heights; finally, the silver-plated cocktail shaker, well used, well loved (because martinis were her drink of choice, always), now so badly tarnished that the monogram of my mother's initials looks like a crooked scratch across the finish.

My mother housed all of this glass in The Bar, an icono-graphic, highly varnished walnut affair with thick, spotlit glass shelves along the wall and a black leather bolster across the front. When I was a child, The Bar was a rarely used area of the family room that looked out on the backyard. By the time I finished junior high, my parents had divorced, the pool had replaced most of the lawn, and my mother had put in French doors to open the family room onto the patio. My mother was like a workhorse back then, her appetite for parties, though she had few friends, driving her like one of those faithful creatures that walk the same furrows every day because they love the work so much, or because there's little else to do.

The summer I turned thirteen she began inviting her poor relations over for "swimming parties." On one occasion, her sister Olga and Olga's husband, Oscar, the meat cutter, sat uncomfortably in the gingham-backed kitchen, smoking and drinking beer, while my mother sailed back and forth from the pool to the table, something iced and highly alcoholic in her tinkling glass, her gold sandals snapping against the bottoms of her narrow, brown feet to the rhythm of Sinatra on the record player. My cousin, Jimmy, slumped in my father's green leather armchair, his dirty jeans and motorcycle boots giving off a gritty smell of motor oil. "For God's sake, honey," my mother said, stopping by his side, "use a coaster." And she handed him a pink Lucite circle to put under his beer.

I sat silently on the couch—wrapped in a faded Snoopy towel and wearing a damp, polka-dot tank suit, hair plastered to the sides of my fat face—shivering and watching. Jimmy was my only cousin. He waited until my mother left the room then pinched cigarettes from the lacquered box on the coffee table with the concentration of a surgeon picking shrapnel from a wound. It was that same singular precision that cost Jimmy his life in a liquor store robbery on the South Side a year later: Once he saw the money he was blind to caution; he got shot by the owner while artfully assembling each pile of bills at the bottom of a paper bag.

For Jimmy's funeral, my mother wore a black linen dress and silk pumps, carried a black straw bag. She stroked the upswept hair at the back of her neck so she wouldn't cry. "Does my slip show when I sit?" she asked herself, pulling at her dress. "Did you shine those shoes, Sandra?" she asked me without looking in my direction.

In the front pew, Olga and Oscar tilted their doughy, pink faces to the minister. Behind them sat several of Jimmy's buddies, bulging and awkward in their polyester suits, hair curling over their collars, acned jaws working gum.

The minister went on about diminished lives, those cut down in their prime. But they didn't *have* to be diminished, I thought. Clearly my mother, who nearly glowed beside me, knew something that the rest of my relatives didn't, for, unlike them, she had a house and a great many possessions, and she knew how to care for them. Some piece of knowledge had fallen to her, and it was hers to nurture and cherish. I wanted this same power, so I vowed that day to watch carefully how my mother kept the world running, how she employed her possessions to achieve the grace of a smooth and even life. Jimmy didn't have this strength. Jimmy didn't have many things—that's why he had gone to such lengths to get them.

When my mother and I came back from the funeral, our house seemed bigger than the church: straining at the walls with heavy furniture and marble table lamps, laid over with thick carpeting, everything clean and operating, the whole downstairs full of the scent of my mother's lilac bushes outside the window. As we sat in the family room that afternoon, sniffling and talking idly about mundane subjects, I felt something in me reverse: The tiny craft that had been speeding through me for years—carrying me from dependence to independence and on to adulthood—had stopped and was now prepared to take me back. I would never leave this house, I told myself, because only here could I learn my mother's secrets, avoid Jimmy's fate, embrace all the objects surrounding me that my mother presented.

Attentive, the tears resting in her eyes, my mother concocted her martini. Like a scientist she lifted, then examined, the bottles, the shaker, the glass. These things are yours, her movements said. All you need is in them.

A LARGE LEATHER ADDRESS BOOK. Tan calfskin, dictionary size, thick, the pages cream-colored and trimmed in gold, the front bearing a monogram, also in gold: DCM, David Charles Millan.

When I was twelve, my father left without a fight, without much noise or warning, in the middle of the night, carrying his extensive wardrobe to the car in leather suitcases and cardboard cartons. My mother helped him. I know because I watched them from my second-floor window. The crickets sawed away, a thumbnail moon sliced across the trees on the horizon—it was the perfect night for a backyard party. My mother and father laughed about something as they put the last of my father's things in the back seat of his Lincoln. Staggered piles of boxes crammed the car; in the dark they looked as if they were climbing out of the seats. My mother walked around patting the boxes, adjusting them, while my father watched. Then she kissed my father good-bye, waved, and he was off.

The next morning she sat with me at the breakfast table. Pink roses in a white vase, eggs and bacon and toast on bone china, white frilly place mats, and my mother in a white eyelet robe, her blond hair tied in a yellow ribbon. She looked like she'd slept. "Don't eat so fast, sweetie," she said, pointing at my plate with her cigarette. "We're going downtown later today. Chicago. To the bank."

I tapped my plate with my fork and stared at her.

"What?" she asked. Then, brightening: "Oh, honey, a wonderful thing has happened to your father. You'll never guess."

"You're right," I said, "I'll never guess."

"Your father has fallen in love! Yes, really. Isn't that great! She's a wonderful woman—Janet. You might remember her:

tall, black hair, a terrific figure. She was at our Christmas party last year."

"Do you think I'm dumb?" I asked, my mouth full of eggs. "I saw you last night. You're breaking up, and you might as well tell the truth about it."

"That's what I'm saying, yes. I mean, your father can hardly be in love with two women at the same time, can he? It wouldn't be fair, either to Janet or me. He had to make a choice, and considering your father's happiness, I think he made the best choice." She looked out the window to the backyard full of rose bushes and lawn and perimeter of maple trees. Perhaps she was already planning the pool.

I hated my mother with a piercing righteousness at that moment. It was impossible to tell when she was real. Sometimes she just seemed to be another bright fixture in the house. Maybe my father just forgot about her one day and there was this Janet instead. "What did you do?" I asked, narrowing my eyes.

To my mother's credit, she never cracked. "I didn't do a thing, darling. I think you know that. No one does or doesn't do things to make a relationship work. You feel things and your actions hopefully follow. So it was for your father. For Janet, that is."

"And look," she continued, opening her arms to the kitchen, to the buttery sunlight, the waxed linoleum, my garish finger paintings in frames on the wall, "he could have left us with nothing. Instead, he said he'd take care of us the rest of his life. So many men don't, you know. They just leave. But we have all this."

We did have everything: the house, the big Chrysler, all the furniture and heirlooms, and my father's family holdings, which were considerable as he was an only child like me. And frankly, I never missed him that much. I remembered him as clean-smelling, rather handsome, and quite short, so that he always seemed dwarfed by our huge house. But he wasn't active, like my mother, either in memory or in real life. I marked his work for us by new chairs, rugs, a car. When my father left us, he left his job with the Chicago firm, eventually he left Janet, and he traveled as a vocation, circling the country, dropping into work at various law offices along the way before he finally disappeared when I was safely in college. He called sometimes from La Guardia or Logan, or even O'Hare, and he talked to me over the pay phone about school, boys, clothes, all the subjects he thought I wanted to discuss but about which I had little to say.

Around Thanksgiving the divorce papers came. They sat on my father's leather-topped desk near The Bar for almost a month. One week before Christmas my mother got out the address book, made herself a shaker of martinis, and wrote season's greetings to each person my father had known. She opened each card, flattened it with the side of her hand, sipped her drink, and wrote "Yours, Dave and Evelyn."

"Honey, pour me another drink, will you?" she asked after the fourth card.

"No," I said from the big leather chair, turning my eyes back to my book.

"Oh, you're at that age, aren't you?" my mother said, going to The Bar.

"What age?" I mumbled.

"Your father's age," she said. "Suspicious. Not caring. Ah." She settled back at the desk. But after a few more cards she said quietly, "That's when they cut you."

"What?"

"Read your book. I'm busy." She made another shaker of martinis.

"Don't you think you've had enough?" I asked, never looking up, only hearing the ice, the gin pouring. Actually, I found these sounds reassuring; they meant that my life would hum on as it always had. I'd asked the question because people on TV always asked it at this point in the drama and because my mother's movements had a sharp, shaky edge that scared me. No matter what, she was never out of control.

"Who asked you?" my mother snapped at me. "Do you want to end up with nothing?" She sat down again, ignoring me as she signed cards and sealed envelopes. Then she got out the stamps. She licked each one, placed it on an envelope, then raised her right fist and brought it down with a bang.

"Mama?" I asked quietly. I was afraid to go near her.

Finally, she stacked and straightened her pile of envelopes and slid them off the desk into the wastepaper basket. I watched as she lit a fresh cigarette, dropped her flaming match after the envelopes, then picked up the papers from my father and dropped them in, too.

"Mother!" I screamed, jumping up.

"Good night, honey," she said, rising from her chair, the address book in her hands. By the time she was on the stairs, the flames had appeared over the top of the basket.

"Mother!" I screamed again. "Crap," I said, grabbing the can with one hand. I ran for the French doors, opened them, and then ran across the patio, the fire stinging my fingers. I flung the basket upside down in the snow until it stopped spitting and smoking. I could hear my mother up in her bedroom, singing an old song.

DOGS: TWO. Great Danes, male harlequins, now elderly and arthritic: Kramden and Norton.

We had a routine, that summer when my mother insisted I come home from Madison where I was a freshman in college, majoring in nothing. My roommate was getting married anyway and leaving school, as all my roommates in college seemed to do. A professor had offered me an easy research job, but my mother insisted that I not work and instead stay with her to "have fun." She was right, of course; we did have fun. My four college summers became the best parts of my life, hanging like ripe peaches in my memory, pastel perfect—pink, orange, and gold against a blue sky, never falling.

Every day we got up late, ate, put on makeup, took our time; there was none of that bitter rush that precedes a dreaded task. Then my mother and I slipped into the new Cadillac, blasting cold air, and floated to the bank where my mother withdrew crisp, fresh money.

At the mall, in Marshall Field's, our only stop, we didn't have to say a thing because we savored the same details: the hushed slide of the display case doors, the sound of our heels on the tile, the shine of the lip gloss on the clerks. "Hello, Mrs. Millan," they said. "And Sandra." I got a nod, a puzzled expression: the thick-set daughter following her elegant mother, trailing after an inheritance, they probably thought. What they didn't understand was the shared ritual of our days. My mother and I each bought something small that we wanted, paid for it with our stiff bills, and walked out eating the tiniest Frango bars the store sold.

At home, we'd unwrap our purchases from lightly-scented tissue paper, lay them on our beds or put them in place around the house and admire them, all the while the dogs, yearlings barely out of puppyhood, jumped and woofed around our legs or drank out of the toilet with big, noisy laps. Kramden and Norton had their own room, my old nursery, now filled with enormous bags of dog chow, gaping food dishes that seemed cast from concrete, and two ratty Turkish prayer rugs, the fringe damp and shredded. And now, in summer, the whole house smelled of wet dog: My mother left the French doors open, so Kramden and Norton were in and out of the pool constantly, cooling off their huge, solid bodies—like film stars on an estate, at home, in command.

My mother and I spent the rest of the afternoon in our lounge chairs, sunning, traveling between the pool and The Bar. Kramden and Norton leaped into the pool, heads up, paddling and blowing air, huge jaws biting water, until they were ready to dry. Then they clambered up the graduated cement steps in the shallow end, their great testicles swinging as they struggled like horses out of mud. They immediately ran for my mother and shook off the water, making her shriek.

"Good boys," she said as they settled down like sphinxes between us. Legs straight out in front of them, smacking their lips, they lowered their heads to their paws.

There was usually a sour moment sometime late in the afternoon as the sun sank behind the trees, but it was only a moment. Soon my mother went into the house and came out again with a tray bearing cheese and crackers, the martini shaker, and a cold beer in a frosted glass. The alcohol pushed us over that invisible line again—the one that separated us from worry or loneliness. The house loomed silently over the patio.

We became sleepy. My mother usually dropped off at dusk, snoring quietly, the glass still in her hand, her long, brown legs drooping over the sides of the lounge chair. I rested, but kept one eye on my mother. She seemed to have calmed the world, slowed it down, wrapped it around me, and I felt that if she were disturbed, the earth would shudder in sympathy.

Periodically the dogs lifted their heads and looked toward my mother, then glanced nervously at me. They seemed to be waiting for my mother to give them a signal, though she had never had them trained. They couldn't even be walked, as I learned every time they dragged me around the streets of our suburb. Unlike most other dogs, they were always anxious to get back home.

My mother adopted the dogs because I was gone. "I'm so lonely!" she had said into the phone each week for six months or so, until one time I heard yapping when I picked up the receiver. "You'll never guess," my mother said. After that, it was the dogs this and the dogs that. I didn't really mind; they were dogs, after all. But every detail of my mother's anecdotes spoke of the dogs' devotion to her, their loyalty, their dependence. I was falling behind somehow. Madison began to feel too free and wild, one hundred and eighty miles too far away, until the rescuing summer came and I could join my mother again.

The dogs padded over to my lounge chair and whined quietly, finally sitting next to me. They gazed at my mother, brows wrinkled. Kramden sniffed the air, Norton stiffened his ears; they were on guard. We all were. I sipped my beer while we waited in the hot dark until my mother finally awoke.

"Your brothers," my mother said, her voice rough. She held out her bony hand for them to lick.

A BOX OF ASSORTED SWIMWEAR. Including: five bikinis with matching cover-ups, four tank suits, three newer swimsuits with attached skirts and built-in prostheses, three terry cloth robes embroidered with the crests of various hotels, one pair of men's swimming trunks, and seven rubber bathing caps, one ringed with curls of real hair.

She wore the bikinis and cover-ups throughout my childhood when she was tiny, slim, even muscular from her long walks and the exercises she did along with the TV every morning. The swimming trunks were my father's: navy blue, the words "Chicago Athletic Club" across one leg; he never swam in our pool. The modest tank suits were mine.

The skirted swimsuits, all three, and the curl-fringed bathing cap came from a store in Palm Beach near where my mother took me on a vacation about a year before she died. I was twenty-five, ready to be trained as my mother's caretaker. I spent the first day in Florida holding her elbow, guiding her out of the plane, into cabs and stores and lobbies, finally steering her into our hushed hotel room, the fan ticking overhead.

My mother dressed for the beach the next day as if for battle, slowly, with heavy sighs, her hands shaking. The suit went up over her skinny, brown legs, over her one breast; she positioned the prosthesis over her scar; then I helped her work the tight bathing cap over what little hair she had left. Together, we lined up her pill bottles on the dresser. I whispered dosages as she took each medication from her bag. Then my mother applied her moisturizers and makeup and her sun cream and we were ready to descend to the beach.

We lay, slick and browning, near our rented cabana. Mother was wearing her new yellow one-piece with the attached pleated skirt and her new cap with the curls that looked like eyelashes all around her face. She placed a seashell over each eye.

"You can smell the salt, Mama," I said, opening our tiny cooler to take out the martini thermos and a beer.

Blindly, she lifted her head just a little to sip her drink. Her face was drawn and tense under her makeup, her mouth set in an irritated line. Glancing at her out of the corner of my eye was like watching a movie running on in front of me, a set of small scenes designed to make me remember her. Memories were like this: slips, faults, small gestures loaded with meaning. That was all I wanted—just the opportunity to guess in private about the meaning of my life with my mother. I already knew that as I got older, these poses, these memories, would become pieces of what I thought I'd known all along.

Coming to the bottom of her thermos, my mother began to cry. "Oh, damn," she said, tears squeezing out from the sides of the seashells. "Oh, shoot, now."

"Mother, what is it? Do you feel sick?"

She put both hands on the place where her breast had been and pressed down hard. The rings were loose on her wrinkled fingers, but her nails were still perfect, rounded, frosted pink. "It's coming, Sandra," she said. "I can feel it. Right where it left off, too. You know, where it is, you'd think it was a heart, giving out blood, but it's just there to take me. It'll take me, honey! Oh!" And she pressed down harder, sobbing.

"Mom, jeez." I tucked a terry cloth robe around her legs as if that would help. She was like liquid running out of the shape that usually held her.

"Feel it, Sandra. Sweetie, put your hands here!" And she lifted her own hands off her chest and reached blindly for mine.

"Now, Mama," I said. "I . . . don't . . ."

She grabbed my hands and flattened them on top of her yellow swimsuit. The prosthesis collapsed under my palms, and I closed my eyes in embarrassment. Under my eyelids I saw our dream of a hotel room—plush, scented, quiet, and dark against the sun's glare. Here, I had to watch her cry. It was as if the bareness of the sand, our lack of cover, had brought it out. I was paralyzed by my lack of any appropriate feeling.

"Can you feel the cancer coming out?" my mother asked. "Tell me you can. I'm not that strong. I can't fight this again, you know."

"Mother, shut up," I said, lifting off my hands, but she pulled them back again. "Shouldn't drink in this heat," I added quietly, more to myself.

"I know someone else has to be able to feel this sickness coming," my mother whispered, holding my hands down. "It's got to be you."

I tried but I couldn't feel anything, no death waiting, not the rumble of tumors forming, no blood spurting, not even her heartbeat. There in the coming shadow of the shiny buildings behind us, all I felt was the sun my mother had brought me to see.

A WANT. Not a thudding ache, wanting appeared rather as a jolt, followed by an inevitable change in my life that allowed me to escape from a place where I cared for nothing to a place where too much mattered.

Six months after my mother died I found myself in the kitchen at work with a waitress, Jensine. Three other sullen waitresses in green smocks pushed through the door from the dining room, their angry faces framed in the porthole before they gave a kick and stormed in. Cookie's was the kind of restaurant that employed miserable people. They stayed on for years—sometimes, like Jensine, for a lifetime—just to gripe. It gave them energy. As assistant manager, I was responsible for all trouble, unprotected from all misplaced rage, and uncredited for all success. Jensine held a plate under my nose.

"Sandy, honey," she said. "The dick on twelve returned his dinner. He says there's a hair."

"So give him a new one. Why are you asking me?" I had a long shift that day, so I had filled six pill bottles with scotch instead of three. I fingered four full ones in the right pocket of my cardigan.

Jensine sighed. "Mr. Giaco said no returns without checking first. Remember?"

"No. I don't remember a thing from one day to the next, Jensine," I said, smiling. "That's my plan anyway." Giaco's bald bullet head appeared in the porthole and he pushed his way through.

"What's the holdup here?"

"Hair problem," I said. I couldn't seem to stop smiling. Jensine and Giaco just looked at me. This wasn't work, it was a long list of petty grievances.

Giaco folded his arms. "Jensine, go. A new dinner. Sandy, my office."

I followed him back behind the kitchen, past aluminum tables that held towers of plates and bowls, past the pantry stacked with cans of ketchup, sliced beets, green beans, past the freezers full of beef, chicken, veal steaks. Giaco was ostensibly the man in charge of all this, but he did little besides clap the shoulders and kiss the cheeks of various nameless associates as they made their way to meetings in the banquet rooms. One of them owned the restaurant, Jensine told me. A tax dodge, I told her, knowing money.

It was painful sitting under the lights in Giaco's office, within earshot of the kitchen noises, painful to be so close to anything that kept me separate from my mother's house, even now that she was gone. She had tolerated my job during her final nine months of invalidism, tolerated it just barely, even though I gave her a visiting nurse. "I'm sick," my mother would say every morning as I went off to work, leaving her crying in her rented hospital bed, the gin and chemical treatments surging through her blood. Next to her, on the nightstand, was an eerie still life of her existence: rows of medication, martini makings, an ice bucket, a Styrofoam head wearing a gray wig set in an Ann Landers style. Some mornings, if my mother was too weak to sit up, I would turn from the doorway when she said good-bye and imagine that it was the fake head that had called to me.

"We've got a problem, Sandy," Giaco said, sitting down behind his desk.

At home the walls creaked and sighed, the clocks chimed, the dogs panted. Everything had some meaning, as if, before my mother died, she had left on each of her possessions a card discussing the value of each item and how to weigh its significance. I got this job, and kept it, because that's what people did. They "stayed involved," "went on," no matter what, just as my mother had gone on with her house as long as she could. But all the time I was at work I felt as if I'd left my real life behind at home. Work was like a bad TV show, minus the laugh track. I was surprised, as usual, by how ghostly other people were, how difficult to place, and I was surprised at how uninterested I was in figuring them out. My boss's presence now was as light as breath, irrelevant, as if he were from a land I'd never even imagined.

"I'll get right to it," Giaco said. "I don't like to beat a dead horse."

"What?" I asked. Behind Giaco's desk hung a huge photograph of him kissing the Pope's hand.

"You're on the sauce," Giaco said, his eyes closed.

"Yes?" I asked, waiting for more. For a second I had a familiar feeling, one of fingers tugging at my clothes, an insistent hand that could pull me in a direction, any direction, the way my mother used to.

"Well?" Giaco waited. "I think this needs some explanation."

"Oh, well then I guess I quit," I said, rising, disappointed. "Okay?" I asked, looking back from the doorway. He remained silent as I walked out and left my plastic nametag next to the bowl of moist, crumbling mints by the cash register.

Now I could organize things, I thought, my key scratching at the lock of my mother's Fleetwood. Now I could sort and inventory what I had.

It's not as they say: It's not money that talks, it's the things that money can buy. These things talk loudly; sometimes they yell. I wandered my mother's property with a clipboard and made lists of what was in the house, the garage, the yard. I even have the dogs marked down, though they're probably not long for this world. Kramden and Norton lie next to my chair as if they never noticed that my mother is gone; it's the old leather smell, the scratched wooden legs, the simple shape they cling to. I have accounted for most items on my list, but lately, at night, when the moon comes through the French doors and I pour another drink, I wonder whether I should start over and go through it all one more time, in case I missed something.

MIB

When I was a child and had no sense of anatomy, I believed that my heart lay at the dead center of my chest, between my flat breasts and ringed by bone, open and vulnerable, an easy target. I used to make my best friend Jerry resuscitate me: I would lie down and he would pound on my bony front with his palms until I faked a recovery. Gasp, twitch, flutter my eyes, and I was miraculously alive once again. After a few years I knew better, though. I learned in school that my heart was really hidden under my left breast, and the older I got the dimmer became the sound of my heartbeat, muffled as it was by fat, glands, and tissue. Soon I had witnessed the whole disillusioning science of adulthood that explains and diagrams the magic and pathology of the body and its muscles and organs, and the brain, and even emotions.

But before that I had Jerry. He and I were thirteen, inseparable, and bored–bored enough one summer day to drag a box full of Barbie paraphernalia out to the mudhole beside my family's garage. Jerry had perfected a repertoire of voices for doll doctors, doll lawyers, even a doll priest; I was in charge of the car crash victims. That day I drove Barbie's Corvette over the faces of Francie, Skipper, and Alan as they lay like logs in the mud.

All these props of the doll world came from Jerry's sister. I had my own dolls, but I refused to take them out of their original boxes. They rested in perfect condition, hair coiffed, clothes pressed, behind cellophane windows far back in the darkness of my bedroom closet.

"Careful," Jerry said that summer afternoon. "You're getting Francie's hair caught in the wheels."

"Make Ken the nurse," I said, pressing one of the Corvette's wheels deeper into Francie's rubber head. Barbie sat in the driver's seat, naked, smiling, a .13 alcohol level in her veins, her arms raised like a cheerleader's.

"A nurse. Right." Jerry snorted.

I laughed and sat back on my heels. Anything was possible. We'd had marriages between hapless Skipper and various plastic animals, Ken giving birth to a baby, armed duels between Barbie and freckled Midge. Much later, Jerry would say we were working at something more serious, a ritual for misfits that toughened us for the years ahead.

Jerry hopped Ken over to the line of dolls in the mud. "Stand back, help is here," he said in a deep voice. "Sweetheart," he added.

The back door slammed, and then my older brother, Roger, hulking and beautiful and sixteen, came around the corner of the garage. Jerry looked up at him with wet, sad eyes.

Roger smirked, then jerked his head towards the house. "Mom wants us."

"What for?" I asked.

"You know," Roger said. He walked back to the house, shirtless, a stiff form of shiny muscles moving under the sun. "Robot Boy," I used to call Roger when we were younger. Then he would chase me around the house and out into the yard, swinging his plastic baseball bat at my retreating head with such force that I could feel each whoosh of air on the back of my neck. My family dared me to love them.

"Oh, God, Rhonda," Jerry said, letting out his breath. He was big for his age, filling his tight, white Levis and purple button-down shirt. He had clear, Dresden-doll skin and thick chestnut hair that hung in a clumped forelock above his black-framed glasses. Like a supplicant kneeling in the mud, he gazed up to where my brother had just stood. I hated it when people didn't see things the way they really were and wished for something they'd never have; it made me cruel.

"Will you just forget it?" I snapped. "Roger's got a girlfriend already. He's got about fifty."

Jerry began throwing dolls back into the box.

"I'm sorry," I said. "It's just my mom."

"Sure," Jerry said, not looking up.

"Stay here, okay? I'll be right back." I stood up, planting my left foot squarely on top of the dolls and encasing my tennis shoe in mud. I continued into the house, not caring. I wanted to track mud and leave prints everywhere, like Bigfoot, like some threatening monster you know is around but you can't see.

The light from the TV led Roger and me to our mother slumped in an easy chair in the darkened living room, her empty bourbon glass sitting on the arm. I could have found her with my eyes closed.

"I already ran the water," Roger said, as we bent to lift her up.

Roger's scalp, sweet-smelling and sweaty, hovered near my face as we hooked our mother's arms over our shoulders. Against the fashion, as always, Roger had a crew cut, black and close like a G.I. Joe doll's. He wanted to join the marines to get out of the house, and he hoped Vietnam would last another few years so he could get there and set up jungle traps, kill some enemy. We dragged our mother up the stairs as if she'd been wounded in some battle.

"Stupid kids," my mother said as we paused in the bathroom doorway. "You forgot the bubbles."

"They're there, Mom," I said. "You just can't see them." The water sat flat and gray in the tub, steaming.

"Stupid kids," she said again.

Roger held her up while I took off her clothes and kicked them into a pile in the corner. He averted his gaze the first dozen times we had to undress her, but now he stared hard at our naked mother, at all her parts laid open to his eyes. I think he wanted to will himself numb, or will our mother to disappear.

"Ow," my mother said as she stumbled into the bathtub.

"Okay, Ma," Roger said, "we're going now."

"Fine," she said, sinking down into the water until it reached her nose. I was always afraid she'd drown, but Roger told me to relax, it was all just drama, anyway. When my father came home from work and went upstairs, my mother would rise sober from the cold bathtub, her skin shining, and be his first vision of the evening. After his arrival, she got dressed in fresh clothes, glided downstairs, threw frozen food into the oven, and began round two with her husband. Nothing animated my mother more than a new opportunity to drink.

I stayed in the bathroom and watched my mother until she fell asleep. Then I went to the window and looked down on Jerry where he sat next to the mudhole. I knew he was still hurt by what I'd said. His long eyelashes would be sticky with tears.

I watched the top of Jerry's head, bowed over the dolls; I watched his careful movements as he waited for me. He had taken out the handkerchief he always carried, and he now wiped it over Barbie, then Ken. When he was done cleaning each doll, he flipped up its legs and sat it down. Soon he had a tight circle of tiny, disheveled mannequins, their heads turned to each other as if they were visiting.

*

By the time we were in our late teens, Jerry and I had discovered names for ourselves, other people's names. We knew we were queer, knew what it meant, somewhat knew the consequences. We ate lunch together every day in high school and one day, because of boredom, because of the Chicago cold outside, because of the full moon—who knows—all the other kids chose to pelt us with their leftovers: mashed potatoes, pizza crusts, pieces of hamburger, all in our hair and smeared on the backs of our shirts. Jerry and I giggled on our way to the restrooms to wash off. We knew we had each other.

But it was in the girls' room for me and boys' room for Jerry that we felt our differences. When I pushed open the bathroom door, girls floated toward me across the tile floor, hovered in front of the mirror with combs raised; they turned slowly toward me, inviting me into the girl world, a place I was afraid to enter. I hid in my stall and dabbed at my stained clothes with wet paper towels, Jerry forgotten, and listened to them talking and laughing, their jeans rubbing as they walked, the intimate, cluttered sound as they rooted through their purses. When I came out there were smells: hair spray, cologne, cigarettes, hand cream, and the stale odor of bubble gum like a mask of sugar over my face. The girls stared at me as I washed my hands, and whispered, and some of them smiled shyly at me, the foreigner.

Jerry waited out in the hall, ready to tell me of his uninitiated adventure in the boys' room. A guy brushed up against him at the urinals, staring at his face and then at his crotch; Jerry looked straight ahead. He knew that same boy would call him names some other time, or ambush him at night in our neighborhood and beat him up. People hated us for what we made them think of themselves—it was always that way.

Shortly after that episode, Jerry decided we should give it right back to them and really call attention to ourselves. He would make us clothes—complementary outfits. They were his own designs: flared trousers tight around the buttocks, wide-lapel jackets, and bright shirts with wing collars. We were the only kids who wore suits to school. Overnight, teachers treated us better; they began to respect us and talk to us as if we were colleagues. We even went to the senior prom in Jerry's suits, creating a scandal, short-lived and implosive, like all high school shocks. My parents took pictures of Jerry and me before the dance: Jerry in a light blue double-breasted suit with a fuchsia- and royal-blue striped shirt, me in a cranberry suit and light green shirt, both of us in coordinated flowered ties.

My father sent a photograph to Roger in Vietnam—where he was out of the action, loading ships in a port on the South China Sea, and in the army, not the exclusive marines—and he responded months later with a note on crumpled paper. "Jesus God," he wrote to me. "But I guess I always knew about you, anyway. Tell Mom and Dad I'm not coming home." The pull-out ended a year later and Roger fled to Europe, where he stayed, working at various jobs, not knowing anyone in particular, making sure that little was asked of him, I imagined. After a few years he picked up a Swedish woman, and they had children and circled Europe, pursuing work. Roger wrote to me once a year, on my birthday, always from a different country.

It's false to assume that you learn about love from your romantic relationships, or, even earlier, from your parents. You learn about love from the friends you make as a child, those kids with whom you spend all your time playing, arguing, making up, laughing, telling secrets. They are the first to share your complete life—sometimes the first and the last. That's why I was so despondent when, after high school, after Roger signed up, Jerry went to FIT in New York. But what else could he do with all that talent except leave our suburb and leave me? He became famous after college, a sensation. Clippings fell from his letters: *Vogue*, *Bazaar*, Butterick pattern books, and, eventually, a profile of his new apartment in *House and Garden*.

All of Jerry's clothes were colorful and sexy; they were for women who looked streamlined and tough, who worked great jobs, and who fucked all the time. I couldn't wear any of them. I escaped from my parents' house right after Jerry left for college, and I moved into a Chicago apartment, rattling around in bad jobs for a few seasons until I landed at a bookstore. After only eight years, I had struggled my way to weekend manager and felt that I'd finally gotten lucky. Truthfully, though, I got great satisfaction out of selling books to strangers, each volume like a box containing another's life, with clean-cut corners and hard impermeable covers to close at the finish like lids clicking shut. I read everything—all the returns, the remainders, the sale books—and I gave long seminars over the phone to Jerry about quantum physics, the media and the presidency, the history of Alcoholics Anonymous, and all the plots of bad novels, turgid and fabricated, so unlike my own life.

"What are you *doing*, though?" Jerry asked me one night in the middle of a lecture.

"I'm telling you here," I said.

"I mean, who do you see? Aren't you going out with anyone? What about that Janine?"

"It didn't work out," I mumbled. I couldn't tell Jerry how Janine, exasperated and puzzled, had left me for someone more forthcoming; for someone who, as she said once when we were fighting, "lives here, outside, with the rest of us." I had gone back to the bars for a few months, to the pool tables and the dance floor, but I felt too old now to try to force myself past shyness and terror to talk to anyone, let alone start another relationship. And my friendships formed and disintegrated with my love affairs; I found that I had a wide circle of acquaintances, but no one I really knew well. Now I just watched a lot of old TV shows and read these strange books; I took a scattershot approach to learning more about people and imagined myself a scholar of the human condition. Talking to Jerry made me realize how little I knew. He moved effortlessly among people, planning parties, going on group vacations, and, lately, sharing tragedies. So many of his friends were dying, he had told me, and so many people were angry; they were thinking of organizing. But that night what I really wanted was familiarity—just Jerry's friendship—something I never got enough of as a child.

"Well," I said after a long silence, "at least I've got you."

"Aw, now, honey," Jerry said. "One person won't get anything done."

My parents died within months of each other during the winter Jerry and I turned thirty, their livers so swollen that the skin on their bellies was stretched taut, their faces so raked from the inside by years of drink that they both bore blue- and rose-splotched cheeks. My brother, after my letters found him in Berlin, sent me an arch of flowers spanned by a white ribbon; it looked like something for the neck of a racehorse. "I don't want anything," he said in the accompanying telegram.

I sold my parents' house with most of their possessions still in it, but not before cleaning out all traces of my own tenure there. I thought of Jerry when I found all my old Barbies and their endless outfits still preserved. A collector from Glencoe bought the whole works for almost a thousand dollars. Everything I had was MIB, mint-in-box, the collector informed me in amazement.

"Imagine getting all that money for toys just because you didn't play with them," I said.

"Yeah, I guess," the collector said. "Where did you live as a child, anyway," he asked, "in a museum?"

"Sort of," I answered.

A few weeks later, Jerry appeared on my television set leading a group of men and women in a protest outside a building in Manhattan. Some carried signs shaped like tombstones on which they had printed the names of the deceased and their dates of birth and death. Jerry was singled out by a reporter, and he spoke to me from my TV screen about AIDS, about HIV and ARC and AZT, about all the acronyms. He was breathless and flushed, and he had his hair in a ponytail and wore tiny, round glasses. "We're all here today," Jerry began, and everyone around him cheered, as if being there was the main point. Jerry finished his sentence under the noise, his lips moving in front of the reporter's microphone. The crowd quieted and beamed at Jerry. Then I thought I heard him say: "We've been warned. We've all seen that as people with AIDS die, a lot of free-floating hate is left lingering."

"Oh, God," I whispered to my set. Jerry stood surrounded by smiling faces, but I could see retaliation for this exposure: A punk raising an empty beer bottle to throw, a businessman on a phone cutting off funds. My apartment was dark, hemmed in by other buildings so that the TV screen was like a bright eye looking out at me, judging my isolation. Everyone saw Jerry now; he was local and national, no longer the boy who spoke just for me. Before, he had been the only thing standing between me and others' indifference. Now Jerry himself was a threat, having gone beyond where I felt it was safe to follow.

Jerry's letters still came once a week, but now when they arrived I threw them away without opening them. I walked by my garbage can several times to look at my name and address written in Jerry's hand, and then the letter would be gone, covered up with other trash, and it was too late to retrieve it. Jerry called, several times a week, and each time I'd sit in my chair and let the machine take the call. Jerry's voice went from eager to perplexed, then to angry. "Okay, Rhonda," he finally said, "it's time to move on, I guess. Is that what you're trying to tell me? I'm going now, I'm gone. Remember me fondly," he concluded in a deep, dramatic, doll's voice.

They were coming to Chicago, Jerry and his group, to march, protest, and occupy the ground floor of City Hall. I read about it on a flyer that a woman brought into the bookstore. She had red hair in a crew cut all around her head, except for the silky forelock that hung in her eyes. I put the flyer on my refrigerator when I got home. It was for me alone.

Two weeks later I went to the protest. I heard them long before I saw them—yelps and the hiss of crowd talk and shuffling, and a distorted voice through a megaphone. As I walked toward City Hall, men and women ran past me, most of them in pairs. They were young, they were panting; some carried signs or banners, or the cardboard tombstones I had seen on TV. My hand reached up to touch my hair, shiny and curled and cut like a grandmother's, I now thought, and then down to fuss with the belt on my pressed jeans. I looked the same as I had as a teenager: squat, dark, built like a shortstop. Only now I felt more weary and more sure of being out of place.

When I rounded the corner and saw the square in front of City Hall, I gasped. Men and women swarmed through the space, a block of black T-shirts and signs waving. Chicago police wearing rubber gloves ringed the group. It wasn't until I crossed the street and passed through a gap in the police line that I realized I was going to join the group.

Soon I was deep in the crowd. My hands shook and my eyes stung with tears. Men and women on both sides of me traded off parts of a chant. "Now!" the people on my right screamed, throwing their fists in the air. We moved forward and to the side, in a ripple, funneling ourselves toward the doors. "Now!" everyone screamed. I moved my lips and pushed against the others to get to the front of the group. I wanted to see Jerry, the celebrity, leading the pack. But first I came upon a group of men in wheelchairs. There was no chanting, no sound at all, coming from this front line, just a boundary of silence and the slow movements of the ailing men as they shifted in their chairs or lifted hands to scratch their scalps. Their eyes were wide and moist, and I could see every vein through the tight skin on their faces. I followed as they were pushed and wheeled toward the doors.

Once inside the building, people sat down and I was able to spot Jerry over in a corner being yelled at by a policeman. The checkered headband on the cop's hat flashed up and down as he harangued and gestured to Jerry, who was on the floor hugging his knees. I pushed on.

Before I got to him, he saw me. His mouth dropped open as if in slow motion and he stared, bending his neck back until his face looked right up into mine. He sat on his heels.

"Oh, Christ," Jerry said, shaking his head.

"Hi," I said, sitting down next to him. The lobby was filling up so I had to squeeze beside a woman holding a clipboard and a sign.

"'Hi'? You say 'hi' after nine months of not talking to me? What are you doing here, anyway?"

"Well, I got this flyer. I don't know, Jerry, I guess I came to see you."

"Don't you think it would have been easier to call, Rhonda?" The man next to Jerry snickered.

"I know. It would have been easier to do a lot of things," I said.

"Miss Regrets," Jerry said, sighing. But he smiled and I felt hopeful.

"I kept thinking of us as kids, all the way over here," I said, launching in.

"That's the problem. We're not kids anymore. Look at where we are."

"I know," I said. "What I meant was that I remembered us as kids, and I missed it."

"What did you miss? Your crummy family?"

Jerry regretted that right away. He looked around at the rest of the crowd, at the line of cops that had also entered the building, so I couldn't see his face.

People around us had begun to chant, so now I shouted. "I missed the way we used to be friends," I said. "It was the only smooth thing in my life. It was the only thing I had that was in the open."

"Nothing was open," Jerry said. "That was another problem."

"Want to know a secret?" I yelled, my voice breaking. "All the friends I've tried to have since we were growing up have been inadequate because they weren't you."

"Honey, I'm sorry, but that's no secret."

"Really. Everyone comes up short, even me." I laughed. "It's a big disappointment," I added.

The crowd had grown stiffer and sweatier, shouting, chanting, raising their fists, their mouths stretched wide open, the skin under their eyes dark with fatigue. Jerry didn't say any more to me; instead he turned his face away from mine. "Funding!" he began to yell, along with the rest of them on our side. "Now!" the other side answered. My own family would have ridiculed these people, exposing their infirmities and vulnerabilities in public. We preferred to live closed up, miserable. I saw my mother setting her hair in the bathroom, a glass of bourbon on the Formica vanity, a cigarette's scratchy smoke haloing her head; I saw my father sitting with the family at the kitchen table, his chin slipping from his cupped palm, his elbow from the table, while we all ate TV dinners from foil trays; I saw my brother, his dark eyes burning, stalking an invisible enemy through the backyard with his plastic machine gun. And then there was Jerry: his boy's sinewy arm slung around my shoulders, his low whisper in my ear as it laid out revelations, confidences, a recognition of me as someone to cleave to, someone worthy. It didn't matter what words Jerry used when he talked to me. This is good, this is good, the voice would say, no matter what, this is love.

Everyone screamed now, even me, and we all doubled over in effort down on the floor. My voice came back to me from the walls along with a hundred or more other voices. The policemen conferred, shifting back and forth on their feet. Startled city employees—men and women in suits holding briefcases

—stood behind the cops, the *O*s of their eyes and mouths slowly widening.

"Want to know a secret?" Jerry yelled in my ear. "I'm positive," he said.

"About what?" I asked.

Jerry looked at me. "Jesus, Rhonda! HIV positive."

I nodded again, biting my lip and looking away. The chanting escalated in volume and frequency; men and women hunched their shoulders as if dodging a coming blow. The circle of police grew tighter. The woman beside me was hauled away. As she slid past, she handed me her clipboard and sign.

"You're in charge!" Jerry screamed in my ear.

"Now!" I yelled back, punching the air.

"No, stupid," Jerry said. "You. Our history. You remember it all so well. Don't forget a thing, Rhonda, okay?"

"Okay," I screamed.

"That's better, now," Jerry said.

We both went limp then, and the cops fit their hands under our armpits, lifting us in tandem to carry us away.

Crooks

When I was a senior in high school, in 1975, my boyfriend, Michael, gave me a copy of John F. Kennedy's death certificate.

"Oh, *sure*," I said, when Michael showed me the paper in the yellow circle of his flashlight.

We all stared at it together on that warm May night, Michael, his partner Billy Tree, and me, under the tall, scruffy lilacs near the edge of a quarry in St. Charles. We were waiting for Michael's rich-kid contact to come and pick up the ten stolen CB radios stashed in the trunk of Billy Tree's green Pontiac, which sat about fifty yards away with Lenny, Michael's other partner, at the wheel. Lenny's cigarette lighter flashed on and off inside the car, a sign of his impatience.

The certificate was a bad photocopy, small and black around the edges and blurry, but whoever filled out the form knew history. Date of death, place of death, cause of death: I couldn't help but see the Zapruder film in my head, see Jackie lean over the trunk of the convertible and gather back the top of her husband's skull blown off by the violence, see her try to take some control, salvage what she could; I imagined that the underside of the skull bone was bright pink in the sunlight, strafed by tiny cracks.

I felt unmoored as I stared at the paper, a feeling that sometimes came upon me when I was with Michael and his friends. We stole, broke all sorts of laws; we thought we were iconoclasts, the last of the hippies dying out in the mid-seventies. In my life there was nothing unusual about waiting with my boyfriend to unload hot merchandise, nothing unusual about admiring, as I had earlier that night, Michael's huge chunk of hashish, fragrant as cedar wood. But the death certificate made us hush.

"You don't believe this is real, do you?" I asked.

"Why not?" Michael said. "I got it from Lenny. He got it from his dad. You know Lenny's dad, Ceil."

I did. So did the FBI, the district attorney's office in Chicago, and the Illinois Crime Commission.

Lenny lay on the car horn. "Come on!" he shouted out the window. "This guy ain't coming." Billy Tree waved at him, but none of us moved.

"Shades of the grassy knoll," I said, folding up the certificate and putting it in my pocket.

"What?" Michael asked.

"Never mind," I said.

"Don't do that!" Michael yelled at me. He kicked a rock down into the quarry.

"Hey!" I cried. "What?" The rock made a soft, distant "plish."

"Don't talk to me like that, like you're so superior all the time!"

Michael and I were a good match, I thought: brains and brawn, yin and yang—the perfect complement. But I had been insensitive. This death certificate had been a gift for me,

Michael's bookish honey, and I had ruined it. I grabbed
boyfriend by the shoulders and shook him.

Michael stayed stiff with his hands in the pockets of
denim jacket, his long black hair blowing around his shoulc
"Oh, Ceil," he said, and then poured his bulk right on to
me, almost pushing me over. He hugged me tight into hi
shirt. "You don't know, you just don't know," he whisperec

"Aw, jeez," Billy Tree said, and sighed.

I felt soft yet invincible standing there in Michael's arr
explorer safe and easy in all worlds. I had met Michael
our high school smoking area, and when I joined his gr
friends, so unlike me, they accepted my presence with a l
shrug and resignation. But now I had access, I thougl
love, and I could travel between privilege and criminali
impunity. I relished that power.

Lenny started the car, laughing and flashing the ligh
ning the engine.

"I guess we better give it up," Billy Tree said.

Suddenly Lenny shifted into gear and the car too
ward us, skidding on the dirt and gravel. Michael, Bi
and I tensed in the glare of the headlights like frighte
Just before the car was on us, coming fast, Michael
Tree yelped and dove into the lilacs, scattering grave
quarry. Over the roar of the engine and the frantic s
of the tires as the car came to an uneven halt at my fe
my own high, ecstatic laugh, and Lenny's, and ther
hand slam down on the Pontiac's rocking hood, st(
car dead.

I graduated third in my class that June and wore b
the ceremony, despite a strict prohibition from the
tion. Michael, Billy Tree, and Lenny, soph(
dropouts, sat in the football bleachers. "Fuckii
Michael yelled as I walked across the platform t

diploma. I gave our flustered principal, who, it was rumored, had been caught in a compromising position with a suspended cheerleader, a hug and a kiss on the cheek. I waved merrily to the crowd. We were the largest graduating class in my high school's history—over a thousand kids—the crest of the baby boom set loose in a chaotic world.

That summer my parents gave up on me and let me run without restrictions, staring sadly out at me from the front doorway as I drove away with Michael every day. That summer I also decided that there was something superior in loving someone. You graced your sweetheart with attention, kisses, stories, amusements, sex, and you were aware of what you were doing at every moment. Love was a very clear-eyed enterprise, but full of canniness and caution nonetheless, and no surrender. Michael and I had different ideas about each other and about how and why we loved each other, that I knew. But I also believed that my powers of observation, my vigilance, would pay off in the end. Michael couldn't put anything over on me. I was as watchful and savvy about love as he was about committing crimes.

On a Saturday afternoon a few weeks after graduation, I found myself in a dry field behind the Keyhole Bar in Hanover Park, propped up against a sumac bush while I watched Michael and his friends shoot a pistol at a line of beer bottles.

I had *The Return of the Native* with me, a can of Old Style, and my purse, which still held the familiar detritus of high school: broken cigarettes, cologne bottles, pens, a roach clip, and a fan of blank absence slips that I had stolen from the guidance office months before. Clouds of starlings rose and dropped in the empty fields beyond; a breeze pushed back my long hair. This was the life. Michael, Billy Tree, and Lenny, their backs to me, took turns blasting away with the gun.

"You guys suck!" I yelled.

"Shut up, Ceil," Michael said, taking aim at an empty quart bottle. He missed.

I laughed in my paradise of shade, the sumac leaves slicing the sunlight on my face. Each time the pistol fired the report echoed across the field, ricocheting off the back of the Keyhole. A clean sound, satisfying. Anything off limits had to be worth getting to, I thought, watching Michael's broad back as he took aim. That's what my boyfriend and I had in common.

I noticed a little girl walking slowly through the field toward our spot, pushing the tall weeds aside as she made her way. She wasn't at all curious about her surroundings; she looked straight ahead at her destination—Lenny, Billy Tree, and Michael.

"Jody!" Billy Tree cried. He ran over and hugged her.

Everything about Jody's appearance, from her long, colorless hair and tiny feathered bangs to her twig-thin limbs, made me think of an orphan child, though I knew her from the halls of my high school. Even her clothing was babyish: a powder blue nylon shirt, jeans with red stitching along the sides, and white tennis shoes. She carried a shapeless brown shoulder bag and a huge brass key chain heavy with keys. I could tell, even from a distance, that she was someone who carried no visible presence. Everything was on the inside, hidden power. This was a dangerous person, I thought, the kind of person I always wanted to be. The boys hovered over her as if she had cast a spell.

"That's Ceil," Michael said, tossing his head in my direction. He stared at Jody as if she were a vixen in black leather.

"Hi, Jody," I called out, loud and friendly.

The girl just glanced at me, but she gazed up at all of the guys, liquid-eyed.

Everyone sat down next to me under the sumac where Michael, Billy Tree, and Lenny launched into the plan for their next scheme: stealing back a car they had just sold. I finished my Old Style while I listened to them brag and lie. The humid air lay thick and unmoving around my head.

Jody smiled beneficently and shyly at each one of them,

Billy Tree's skinny arm slung around her, while the boys turned their talk, almost imperceptibly, to her. They softened the details, cut out the violence, deleted the expletives. She pulled them in; she ate up all their secrets. Even I could feel her. Michael, Billy Tree, and Lenny could have been breathing every breath down Jody's throat, they were so into her. She filled herself with them and grew right in front of my eyes.

I got up and walked in circles over the grass looking for the pistol, like a dog searching for a bone. When I found it I picked it up and held it close to my stomach, like a gangster who'd just pulled a heater out of his coat. Then I raised it straight over my head. It was hot and smooth and heavy in my hand. The boys behind me kept talking, planning, planning; Jody, I imagined, just kept smiling. I pumped the gun over my head as if I were doing exercises. Excitement and expectation filled me, and a feeling that I had to make a drastic move, run at the line of everyone's backs and scream like a banshee. Then I laughed softly, thinking: I've been confirmed, for Christ's sake; my daddy is a doctor; my grades are good. I turned and lowered the gun about forty-five degrees and aimed right over everyone's heads.

Firing the gun did not give me the feeling I expected. I was neither thrown on my back nor filled with a jolt like lightning. Instead, only a warm hum shot through my funny bone and then came a thrill, deep in my abdomen. I felt I was in charge of one of the elements. Earth, air, fire, gun; now who was a witch. The bullet went long, skidding through the dirt far from the sumac where everyone sat. I wanted another shot.

"Hey!" Michael yelled. He twisted around. "Put that thing down, goddammit!"

"Watch your ass, sucker!" I yelled and laughed again, as I brought the gun down level with Michael's head. I even supported my elbow with my other hand, like cops do in the movies.

I got out a few more shots that went high, ripping through

leaves and branches; one flaked off some bark over Billy Tree's head. He ducked as the wood sprinkled down on him. "Yeeeow!" I yelled.

I had the physical sensation of my brain almost lurching in my skull, careening happily out of control. I had always believed that people rushed up to a certain line but never crossed it. We all had built-in limits to our behavior, our tastes, no matter how outrageous. But now a new world appeared before me, boiling with opportunities, primeval. I could do anything, think anything. The last time I raised the gun Jody looked at me, startled but still smiling.

"Shit!" Michael screamed, rising to his feet.

I jerked the gun up high again and fired at the hazy sky, the smudged sun. Jody squealed. Michael started for me, furious, then burst out laughing, and, slapping his thighs, fell to the ground in hysterics.

I was the only girl at Billy Tree's apartment in the mornings. Jody never stayed over but left Billy Tree every night promptly at midnight, got into her Gremlin, and drove home before her curfew; afterward, Michael and I would hear Billy Tree tossing and turning in his big, creaky bed in the room next to us. Most mornings that summer Michael and I woke up sweating in the streaming sunlight under Kennedy's death certificate, which was pinned to the wall with a dart. Michael would eventually sigh and rub his hands through his hair and get up to face his empty day, as if he had a thousand pressures closing in. I fell back asleep to the sound of Michael's cough and the click of his lighter under his cigarette.

In late July, the humidity outside thickened and Billy Tree's living room turned cold one night, its air conditioner surging forth under the window. I'd been drinking since late morning in a progressive manner: beer at eleven, rum and Coke at three, and now, at eight, I was sprawled on the floor with everyone else drinking tequila. All the alcohol had pickled me, made me mushy and full of myself.

Michael, Billy Tree, and Lenny had been out all day doing inventory on their small stash of stereo equipment. They couldn't wait to unload it.

"How about those yokels from the football team?" Lenny asked. He passed the bottle and lime wedge to Billy Tree.

"Naw," Michael said, stretching out on the shag carpeting. I stroked his leg; Jody watched me watching Michael. This is how you love your boyfriend, I wanted to say.

"Bikers," Billy Tree said, grimacing from his swallow of tequila.

"Yeah," Michael said. "Perfect. We can use those guys."

"Bikers?" I asked. "Don't they carry guns? Tire irons? Things like that?"

"Bikers don't carry guns, Ceil," Michael said. "Not these ones at least. I know these guys; Russell over at the Keyhole said they've got nothing backing them up—you know. So what." He snapped his fingers.

"Okay," Lenny said, "I'm in."

"Okay," Billy Tree said. All three of them slapped hands.

Michael laughed. "Drink up, kiddies," he said, then he kissed me.

I sighed and bit into the lime. While I was sucking the sour juice I studied Jody. She sat in our circle too, her skinny frame swimming in a tee shirt and bell bottoms that would fit a thirteen-year-old. She drank Dr. Pepper.

"Tequila, Jody?" I asked, holding the bottle out to her. Even I could hear the sneer in my voice.

"No, thank you," she said, barely glancing at me. She turned her attention to Michael again.

I got up and weaved my way to the bathroom and sat there for several minutes, my eyes closing and then snapping open, before I noticed Jody's purse hanging on the back of the door.

I didn't know Jody at all. In fact, I'd never been able to engage her in a conversation. It soon became clear that she was interested only in Billy Tree, or, more to the point, she was interested only in the boys. The curious thing, though, was that she never spoke to the guys and only rarely to her boyfriend. Perhaps the girl communicated telepathically, I thought, as I looked at her nondescript purse holding the mundane artifacts of her life. Perhaps she communicated through high-frequency sounds other girls couldn't hear, like some kind of dog whistle. Bitch. I washed my hands, got the purse off the hook, and sat on the edge of the bathtub.

I found familiar contents in the top layer of the purse: two bottles of Youth Dew cologne, both half-empty; a few broken pencils and a pen from West Suburban Bank, its chain still attached; that massive key chain, which I muffled in my palm. I placed everything on the bath mat. I was breathing heavily from excitement, sweating, my mouth hanging open. Next, I found one of those doggie brushes with metal teeth, so Jody could really go at her hair; a tiny penknife; a large jar of Vaseline; a wallet. At last.

It was a long, grown-up affair with infinite compartments. I counted six dollars and forty-seven cents. Then I pulled out a snapshot and held it up next to my face as I looked in the mirror. It was a picture of Jody with her family: a brother, two sisters, parents, all small, slender, and smiling, dressed for church. They could have been anyone's idea of an American family, stamped out of cardboard. And there I was: face swollen from drink, disheveled hair, panting like a moron. I hadn't been looking too good lately.

Jody's wallet held no notes, nothing really personal, no papers except for a driver's license and a social security card, Jody's signature on it in big, loopy script. Then I unzipped a compartment on the back of the wallet and felt around, finally pulling out three condoms wrapped individually in white plastic. So Jody carried protection, just like all the guys. I imagined her lying motionless under some big, faceless lug, not even thinking of poor Billy Tree, while the guy went at her, her eyes shining up at him in the dark.

I banged around until I found a safety pin; then I commenced stabbing several holes through each condom and its plastic wrapper. The ability to surprise myself with my own behavior was becoming familiar, less fun, and more serious. I poked at one condom so hard the pin went into my fingers on the other side. When I was done I arranged the condoms back in their compartment and replaced everything else in the purse. As I put the purse back on the hook, I saw my shiny face in the mirror again, blurred and churning. A transitional face, I decided, not knowing the transition.

Late on the night of August twelfth, I got out of Billy Tree's car along with Michael, Jody, Lenny, and Billy Tree, and pushed hard against a section of broken chainlink fence near the front gate of a Cook County forest preserve until it collapsed. We all piled back into the car and Billy Tree drove over the fence, the bumpy grass, the curb, and down onto the road that took us back to the dark trees, the picnic areas, and the two bikers, waiting with their cash and their big hogs for the stereos.

It was Michael's Yalta, in a sense. On this night we would celebrate our joining of forces, our peace. Lenny and I got out of the back seat with several cases of beer. Billy Tree had an ounce of good pot. Jody, who was apparently in a foul mood—her quietness was raw at the edges, and I'd seen her refuse to hold Billy Tree's hand—immediately sat down at a picnic table and opened her Dr. Pepper.

I had three beers in quick succession while I inspected the biker's transportation.

"Vrooom," I said, laughing, as I sat on one motorcycle, trying to reach the handlebars. "Jesus, this thing is a monster."

"Want a ride, sweetheart?" Douglas, the bike's owner, asked.

I looked over at Michael, who was going through Billy

Tree's trunk, our showroom, with Foster, the other biker. It was dark in the woods but bright enough, with the lights of the suburbs around us, to make out shapes and movement. I could identify jerking forms and the still, mysterious outline of Jody, silent at her picnic table. I wiggled my fingers at her and smiled from my place on the back of the hog.

"What about it?" Douglas asked, moving up close to me. He was tall and overweight, his fat well-distributed, and he had slicked-back, frizzy hair and black plastic-frame glasses, like a thuggish Allen Ginsberg. Chains on his boots and across the chest of his sleeveless denim jacket clanked when he moved.

"Naw, I don't think my boyfriend would like it." I looked away. "Vrooom," I said again, and laughed.

Douglas swung onto the bike behind me. He grabbed my hands and stretched me far forward until I touched the ends of the handlebars. "See, it's easy. All you need is a little help. What's your name again?"

"*Douglas*," I said, short of breath.

"Douglas is *my* name."

His chain pressed into my back and I smelled him—cigarettes and beer and Brylcreem. He breathed on my neck, the side of my face.

"Douglas, really. I've got to go."

He leaned harder. Something pricked my shoulder, then again. Then Douglas bit down hard, pulling up the fabric of my shirt and holding it between his teeth.

"Grrr," he said, shaking his head.

"Hey, cut it out," I said weakly.

"Cut it out!" Douglas cried in a falsetto. "You big brute! Hey, hey," he said, reaching into his pocket, "you ever see one of these?"

He brought forward a small, silver, lozenge-shaped object and held it between his fingers while he mashed down my hand again.

"What is it?"

The object clicked and a long blade shot out.

I felt an opening of possibilities, of immunity, of wild freedom, of clean, decisive movements with careless intent. Michael and his friends, these bikers, they could all be in jail by next month. And soon I would be in my dorm room at Northwestern, perhaps pulling out the knife to show my new friends, snapping it open in their scrubbed, freckled faces. "Give it to me, Douglas," I said.

"What?"

"The knife. Give me the knife." I pulled my hand out from underneath Douglas's big paw and held it out. At the same time I pushed against him, just enough.

"What're you going to do with it?" he whispered in my ear, pressing back.

"I need it to remember you by."

Douglas let out a wheezy, hiccupy laugh. "Okay, babe," he said, closing the knife and handing it over. "It's our little secret."

"You bet," I said, ducking and sliding off the bike.

The simplicity of Michael's life amazed me. The knife, which I rolled in my palm as I walked away from Douglas, would do several select things, no matter who was holding it—frighten, hurt, kill—but it would always get something done. Nasty business was the great equalizer—anyone could engage in it, and therefore be generally bad. Not everyone could be a good person just by doing a good deed. At least not always. I put the knife in my pocket. Then I stopped in the middle of the picnic area, threw back my head, and howled like a dog. All the guys laughed.

I slid onto the picnic bench next to Michael and across from Jody, stopping the girl in mid-sentence. I wanted to cram something in that little mouth she was running at my boyfriend.

"Stop pushing, Ceil," Michael said, shoving me over to the edge of the bench.

"Hi, boyfriend," I said, kissing him. "What're you guys talking about?"

"Nothing," Jody said sullenly.

"So, did you get a good deal on the stereos?" I asked, turning to Michael.

Michael rolled his eyes. "What are we here for?" he said. Jody laughed.

"I guess to see you act like a shit, Michael," I said quietly. He looked like he was going to yell at me, but then he softened. "Aw, honey, how can you say such a thing to your old man? You're a smart girl, can't you figure out the way I love you?" He and Jody both laughed.

Michael put one arm around me and snaked his other arm across my belly, his hand stealing up under my tee shirt. "My baby, my baby, my baby," he sang, grabbing my breast as he watched Jody's reaction. She looked back, amused.

I could pull out my knife, drive its blade into the picnic table, make some point about what I thought was going on, but I didn't know what was going on. This wasn't about Jody, this wasn't about Michael. And there was a new twist: none of the solutions I had learned from my months with this crowd would work here. I elbowed Michael and he let go. "I'll be with Lenny," I said, standing up.

I joined Lenny in the front seat of Billy Tree's car where he was drinking and playing the radio. We danced in our seats, laughed, and drank a few more beers. I felt some kind of kinship with Lenny because he was also removed from Michael's business. He was passing through like me, waiting to enter his family's business, so secret and blind, lethal, I imagined. I tried to ignore Michael and Jody, but I had a sour, defeated feeling in my throat thinking of them talking about the things I wanted to talk about. Jody looked down, picking at her clothes. If I came at her with my knife, she'd squeak like a mouse, probably cry.

I got out of the car and walked past the table, past the bikers drinking beer, out of the picnic area, until I had to push my way into the trees and bushes. For a long time I sat on a rock and smoked cigarettes and swatted mosquitoes.

I also closed my eyes and thought of my bedroom at home, rose-colored, bedspread and drapes, with a deep red carpet. I had a phone, and books, books everywhere, most of them read. The room waited in my mind, quietly, a breeze stirring its sweet air. I imagined lying on the smooth surface of my bed, my eyes closed, my whole body light, while I worried about the world going by without me.

A makeshift path of tramped-down weeds led me farther into the woods. A breeze was up, pushing away the humidity and closeness and clearing the sky, and bringing from the ground a thick, rich scent of spent foliage.

The path gave out in a mess of brambles, which I pushed through, scratching my arms and snagging my jeans in the process. Once I gasped and jumped because I thought I saw someone behind a tree. And then I remembered my gift. I walked a few steps more until I was between two young maples. I stood listening, then pulled out my knife and snapped it open. There was a siren, far away on another road. I raised my arm and fired the knife at the trunk of one of the trees. I walked over and pulled it out, then turned and threw it at the other tree. Long ago, when I was just a freshman and new to the smoking area at school, people played an initiation game called "chicken." Standing with legs wide apart they threw a switch-blade toward each foot, getting as close as they could without stabbing their toes. I got out of playing, still passing through to the confused world of the accepted, by cracking jokes full of fancy language. The smoking area kids wrinkled their brows and laughed just the same. I was far beyond that now.

There was a much larger tree about fifteen feet away. Closing one eye, thinking hard of success, I shot the knife into the dark.

It fell way short of the trunk, sailing instead into some

bushes around the bottom of the tree. The knife turned as I picked it up from the ground and its blade sliced my palm. Blood ran in a quick line down to my wrist. "Oh, Jesus," I whispered, as I ran back to the picnic area holding my hand and the knife.

I heard the motorcycles revving up before I even got to the clearing, and by the time I pushed through the last bush Lenny and Billy Tree were getting on behind the bikers in a great rush. Billy Tree's trunk gaped open, the stereos still inside; beer cans lay everywhere; Michael and Jody were nowhere in sight. Then, out on the main road, beyond the trees through which the bikes were now roaring, I saw the bright cherry revolving. I heard shouts, and a car door slam.

Without hesitating, I turned and ran back into the woods, crashing through weeds and stumbling over roots. That automatic click, so ingrained, that regulates behavior from the time we are infants, told me not to run with an open knife, but I ignored it. When are those rules no longer applicable? Or are they always part of that base of knowledge that will get one through every trouble unscathed? Now I had come to a place, I was sure, where all rules were irrelevant.

When I got into the darkest trees I stopped and listened, panting. No sirens, no sound of a chase. The motorcycles must have gotten away. Maybe the cops were searching the clearing. I crept on slowly, then stopped again.

There was a rustle to the right of a tree, some quiet squeaks. I moved toward the noise, parted some bushes, and looked down.

They were like two young animals, naked and squirming together in a pile. Michael's long hair hanging down as he scrambled into his jeans, Jody slipping on her shirt. She stopped dressing for a second and looked straight at me, her tiny face tilted up to mine, her eyes like opaque beads in the darkness.

"Hey," I said in a whisper, my voice stiff.

"Shit, shit, shit," Michael chanted, grabbing the rest of his clothes.

"Hey!" I finally yelled. I shook the bushes that separated Michael and Jody from me. And then over and over again I was yelling and crying, the knife dangling useless in my hand. By my third yell, Michael and Jody had picked up their clothes and were gone into the woods, escaped like the rest.

My cries succeeded in attracting two policemen, who came crashing through the woods behind me and found me standing with an open switchblade. I turned as they caught me in the glare of their flashlights. This was the kind of light that would follow me to the police station, then to my home, even on to college, where I would be forever squinting and cringing under someone's scrutiny, never quite measuring up, never quite fitting in. I watched as the cops ran for me in their big shiny shoes, their holsters creaking, their hats bright white in the gloom.

Solved

The guy who put the handcuffs on her was almost as big in the belly as she, and he stunk of cigarette ash, so the moment he touched her she immediately lost the incipient maternal scent of her unwashed hair and body. These days she had a feral odor, like the smell from a twisted rag in the corner of her parents' garage years ago in which she'd found seven pink, pulsing baby mice.

The late night air outside her building was close and insistent like sweaty palms on the back of her neck and the small of her back, more directive even than the two hands that guided her into the backseat of the waiting minivan. The smoker sighed when he got into the driver's seat. He had acne scars and sprouting whiskers. His assistant, a brown-skinned boy with a buzz cut, sat in the passenger's seat. They reported her found on the radio.

It was so simple to be caught: She had answered "yes" to the

question "Solveig Harrison?" and the bounty hunters had
turned her around right in the doorway to her apartment,
adding one of her swollen wrists to each circle of the cuffs. I'm
a wheelbarrow, Solveig now thought as the van bumped over
potholes, I'm just useful parts. Bent over, my arms back and together like handles, my pregnant belly the deep well of the
body, my concave back the opening. I can carry you, her body
said, carrying the baby and more. Carry me on this, darlin', the
baby's father had said when he cooked up the check fraud
scheme. He was somewhere more important now.

The smoker tossed two business cards onto the seat next to
her. One read, "American Eagle Bounty Hunters—We Pick
Up and We Deliver." Underneath the slogan an eagle wearing
a bandanna pushed a stick figure behind prison bars with its
wing. The other card, just words, she already had, somewhere
in her wallet:

Nestor Margolis

Bail Bonds

Let Me Help You out!

"Remember your friend there?" the smoker asked, his finger wagging over the back of his bucket seat.

"You've been in arrears," the buzz-cut boy said happily,
snapping his gum.

"I know it," Solveig whispered. She felt a deep and sudden
sense of guilt tugging her abdomen, a sensation all out of pro-
portion to what she'd done. Just for a moment, she let her head
drop down as close to her lap as it could go. It dangled like the
head of a sunflower.

Addison never looked so ugly as it did at night, a little bit of
the worst of Chicago transferred to the suburbs. Rows of concrete butter dishes filled with apartments, clusters of arc lights
that shone with a nauseating yellow glow, even a pair of rats
scurrying under a cyclone fence in front of the Chevy dealer on

North Avenue. Passing a row of bungalows, Solveig saw the
same man's bluish face on three mammoth TV screens through
three successive living-room windows, convulsing in the same
laugh: again, again, again. Three fractions of movement made
one perfect gesture, complete at the end of the triad of images.
Everything was a piecemeal job, even an emotion. Everything
took practice, trial and error—or just error. For example, say
you hooked up with the same kind of man over and over again:
the kind who was gone. Or say you sat at the little kitchen table
until late at night practicing someone else's signature long after
the baby's father had gone to sleep, trying so hard to fold yourself into another life, one with money this time, one to support
another mouth. The bounty hunters' radio whistled and sang.
"Over," a woman's voice said, then said again. The smoker
turned off the air and lowered Solveig's window.

They drove past a tavern on Geneva Road. Solveig squinted
at two men in the parking lot; maybe that tall, rangy drunk was
the baby's father. Or not. The van rocketed past under a tepid
half moon.

When Solveig was a girl, she thought the sun and the moon
were the same heavenly body; the sun rested when it became
the moon, then returned as cranked-up daylight. Night and
day had the same swollen feeling, but it was the moon's shyness, its incompleteness, that gave night its mystery. She and
the baby's father were too much the same, finally, both too elusive and masked, both too much night, really. And a full life
equals both sun and moon, she thought, passing under the
pulse of street lamps, both light and dark, known and un-
known, halves of an equation she had never solved.

In Wheaton, near the courthouse, in the elevator going up
to Nestor Margolis's office, the smoker signed off on the paperwork. He folded the thin pink sheet and then, smiling,
swept it back and forth in front of Solveig, looking for a place
to put it.

It was simple: She wore a huge blue gingham maternity

dress with patch pockets. She stuck her belly in the bounty hunter's face. But the captors were always stupider than the captives. The baby's father claimed that crooks got locked up not for transgressions but because they were smarter than everyone else—the authorities simply hated the competition. "Put it in my teeth," Solveig finally said to the smoker, snapping down in the direction of the paperwork. "Animal," she added.

"What a joker," the guy said, handing the pink slip to the boy. "And nothing to joke about, right, Griffin?"

The elevator door opened on Mr. Margolis hiking up his pants, a cigarette in his mouth.

"William, for crying out loud, take those cuffs off," he said to the smoker, who led Solveig to the bondsman's office door. "Can't you see she's with child?"

"It's just the rules," Solveig said, smiling full-faced at Mr. Margolis while the bounty hunter worked on her wrists. She hadn't remembered the bondsman's being so small and rabbity and dark. The baby's father said Margolis was Mexican, but he looked like he had the same narrow, European features of Solveig's own ancestors under his berry-brown skin. He had wavy hair, too, and luminous eyes that seemed far too hopeful, given his profession.

She dropped into the chair in front of his tan metal desk.

"It says on your file here 'Solved Harrison,'" Margolis said, chuckling and scratching at the mistake with a skinny blue pen. "But we've got nothing solved, have we?" He tapped the file. "Where's your friend, Solveig? He was supposed to help you ante up on the bond."

She cursed quietly as her eyes misted over. Gone, subtracted, he was.

Margolis had a tan file cabinet to match the desk to match the file folders bearing the names of those beholden to him. Behind his desk chair was a folding table on which sat a typewriter and office supplies. In the center of the table, presiding over a display of pencils and boxes of paper clips, was a series of framed photographs of an enormous woman with blond curly hair like a child star's, smiling away in a set of brightly colored dresses that progressed in style to the present day. Unchanged was the woman's sunny face beaming out at Nestor Margolis's back as he swiveled slightly in his black vinyl chair, waiting for Solveig's answer.

That woman likes her size, Solveig thought, admiring her heft, her roundness, her fullness—the better to take up more space in the world. There were no other photos in the office, no pictures of children with the woman or with Margolis, just this glorious, grinning blonde. Golden hair, pearly teeth, creamy skin. She shone like the sun from behind Margolis's desk. June bugs banged against the screens of Margolis's office windows as if to get at her light.

Solveig suddenly felt the bugs' urgency, coupled with wooziness, as if she had sucked in all the air around her. Great size had its own perfection and grace, she thought, casting her eyes back to the photos of the woman, perfection and grace like the enormity of the planets and stars exploding from their trapped distances and rushing thin, delicate light to earth. Behind closed eyes, Solveig saw Margolis's wife and herself rotating on opposite ends of space, Solveig curled into her own body like the fetus inside her, the wife gesturing to her, a smiling orb with empty arms askew. Solveig began laughing at this image as she heard Mr. Margolis say, "We'll work with whatever assets you have, dear girl."

She had more assets than he knew, she thought, laughing harder as the perfection of her idea took shape. She stroked down her belly, still laughing. She laughed until her water broke, right there on the blue Naugahyde chair in the bondsman's office. The surprise made her whoop and laugh even louder. Before the fit of laughing quit her, Nestor Margolis was on the other side of his desk wearing a low-slung smile, no surprise in his face, his small, brown hands as soft as fur gloves grasping her arms and helping her down to the gray nubby carpeting to prop her against the front of the metal desk. Solveig spread her legs and lifted her dress to show the dark crown of what she had to give, what she had for payment. Her body emitted the smell of blood and iron and sour milk.

Solveig stared hard at Nestor Margolis. Here was the other part of every crook's equation for getting out, the man who owned the sun. That hopeful look, she thought: Margolis must rejoice in the sight of people freed, blinking in the outside light; and he must rejoice in the woman he married, whose great body shone out at people like a gilded dare. But Solveig saw in the repeated photos and in the bondsman's searching manner that he held only half of the firmament.

It was simple: When Solveig felt the first tearing lurch inside her body, she pushed furiously, eager to release the baby she would hand over like a full moon to the dark of Nestor Margolis's waiting eyes.

The Money Stays, the People Go

§

Hector's lawyer was big. He filled the whole doorway, but not with fat, thank God. He was muscular and very tall and seemed to be only a few years older than my boyfriend, Billy Samms, who was twenty-seven. He gave me an idea of what a man that age who had a good job would look like. The lawyer had a great pile of blond hair and sleepy, mysterious eyes like Robert Mitchum's, one of which he winked at me. Billy was cuter, but he was rather scrawny. Even his black, wispy hair flew about, uncontrolled by anything important keeping it to his head. The lawyer's appearance seemed to follow strict rules. His odor of Brut and cigarettes bored its way across the motel room toward me.

Billy and I had traveled from Los Angeles to Las Vegas, but not to gamble. I had taken time off from work for what I thought was a foolish trip to the desert so Billy could pick up some money. Billy, the only male left in his family, had inher-

ited an undisclosed sum from his late Uncle Hector, a junk
dealer who had his headquarters somewhere near Las Vegas.
All we had to do, Billy kept reassuring me, was take a bus into
town, grab the dough, say thanks to Hector's lawyer, and beat
it. Chronic unemployment can make a man cocky, or just stupid. I knew it wasn't going to be that easy, from the looks of this
hunky lawyer. He was no simple case.

"Cecil Jackson," the lawyer said to Billy, who pumped his
hand like a country fool. I could tell Billy admired the guy, too.

"I'm Tracy Klosowski," I said, then laughed nervously and
dropped my hairbrush. It was hopeless, I decided, glancing in
the mirror again at my snarl of red hair. I saw Billy and the
lawyer behind me, stiff and patient, waiting for something to
begin. Cecil smiled at me again and snapped his gum. "Forget
it," I said. "Let's go."

Cecil had a Lincoln Town Car, glowing in the desert night,
loaded with options and brand new. It was black with red seats
that I sank into like they were my lover's arms.

"This reminds me of a plane," Billy said. "We took Grey-
hound." He paused. "We don't have a car yet. We're saving up
until I'm able to go back to work." Billy's long legs buckled
against the dash.

"How is L.A., Billy?" Cecil swung the car out of the motel
parking lot. The drive was so smooth I could have sworn Cecil
was just pushing the car with his huge hands.

"Not good, not good at all. I can't get any kind of work, not
even construction. And I'm always looking." This was news to
me.

"You should move here," Cecil said. "They're always building. And there's always money. The economy's looking up, you
know. Way up."

"I stayed here for a week once and that was enough," Billy
said. "Every morning I would get up and I'd have nothing
—money-wise, that is. Gone. I thought there was a huge river
underneath Las Vegas with all the money from chumps like me

running through it. Direct lines coming from all the slot machines and so forth. No thanks."

We stopped in a parking lot off the downtown area. I could see the brightest lights glazing the black sky just a few streets ahead. Cecil took us down Fremont Street where Billy and I peeked into gambling houses and restaurants with slot machines. Cecil kept a little bit ahead of us, smiling and nodding to people we passed. He was a commanding figure: those cushioned eyes, cowboy boots, a black suit covering his bulk. He wasn't dwarfed by the lights the way Billy and I were.

We entered the lobby of the Golden Nugget where Cecil led us under endless chandeliers and over miles of marble tile to the Victorian Bar. I held Billy's hand. This was some kind of sleazy heaven and I was just a shuffling rube.

Wanda, our cocktail waitress, had a confectionary hairdo that towered over her skimpy uniform. Billy, Cecil, and I were dazzled. Cecil knew her, of course, and he squeezed her long-fingered hand. She had on a wedding ring, the diamond turned into her palm.

"Wanda's my girl," Cecil said, smiling at Billy and me.

"And I wonder how often Cecil says that without substituting some other gal's name," Wanda said, pulling her hand away. "Hi, sweetie," she said to Billy, ruffling his hair. He grinned up at her. "And what'll you have?" Wanda bumped Cecil's shoulder with her ruffled hip. He lit up a Kent.

"Now this party's on me, so you order up," Cecil said. "Wanda, I'll have my usual."

"Check," Wanda said. She turned to me.

I watched Cecil shift his cigarette from one hand to the other. Even inside the lights were bright and hot. "Billy and I'll have the same as Cecil," I said.

"Wonderful!" Cecil cried. He shooed Wanda away.

I settled my butt into the soft booth. Two men in three-piece suits sat at another table. Their waitress looked remarkably like Wanda, except that her stack of hair was orange instead of white blond. The two men smiled up at her and one of them gave her a folded bill. The waitress tucked the bill up into her hair.

"Cecil," Billy began, "I'd like to talk about my inheritance. Tracy and I are barely making it. I'm especially worried because Tracy's expecting." He patted my arm. "A baby."

I gasped, then started coughing, waving away Billy's offer of a napkin while I kicked his leg under the table. Cecil stared straight at me, smiling so hard I could barely see his eyes. I felt naked, set loose in a strange field without direction. "That's right," I said suddenly, shifting to attention, "I'm going to have a baby." Why not, after all? "In a few months I'll deliver," I continued. "Probably about six. That's what caused me to put on this weight. I used to be skinny." It suddenly mattered how Cecil saw me.

"A stick," Billy said.

"A baby!" Wanda had arrived with our drinks. "Isn't that nice, Cecil?" She moved up close to Billy and set down his glass, the ruffles from her costume brushing his nose. "Bull's eye," I heard her whisper in Billy's ear.

I grabbed my sweaty glass and took a huge gulp. Actually, I already felt drunk. The business suits at the next table laughed at something the waitress was telling them. Cecil smiled away at me, his eyes glinty, his cigarette poised in his meaty hand.

"Personally, I'm in favor of babies," Cecil finally said. "If everything's laid out properly they're wonders. Congratulations." Wanda moved off. I gulped some more of my drink.

"That means we really need the money," Billy said. "And we need good counseling. Investments, tax shelters, you know."

Cecil just smiled and nodded, nodded and smiled. "No, I know how the little joys can turn into little burdens," he said. "We'll work all that out. Later. Drink up, I'm ordering another round."

I splashed some of my new drink in a tiny puddle on my lap. "Ooops," I said, and giggled. I felt a stirring, way down in my abdomen. One of the business suits watched his waitress while the other drew something on a cocktail napkin. The waitress pointed to her right, her other hand on her hip, and smiled at both men.

Cecil said, "Time to throw around some money. We can play whatever you like. Myself, I'm a craps man."

Three more gin and tonics appeared in front of us, with limes the size of lodestones. "For the ride," Cecil explained.

"I'm with you, Cecil," Billy said, puffing himself up next to me. "Tracy, give me some money."

"Are you crazy?" I asked.

Billy held out his hand and waited. I gave him thirty dollars from my wallet.

"Billy and I will go to the crap tables," Cecil announced, watching Billy pocket the money. "Will you be all right? We're going to talk business."

"I guess," I said. "I'll try the slots."

I strolled amongst the slot machines looking for the one that would speak to me. I finally settled for one next to a woman of about forty who was playing for all she was worth. I put in a quarter, closed my eyes, and pulled the lever. Oranges, lemons, and cherries flashed by.

"If I'm lucky," the woman said, "my good-for-dirt husband will forget I'm here and I won't have to go home with him. Maybe he'll tell the kids to forget me, too."

The woman never took her eyes off the machine. I loaded another quarter.

"He's in love with my sisters," she continued. "Both of them. He says it's easier just to stay in the family with me, with someone he knows, than to get a divorce and choose between the sisters. He's always liked my family."

"What do your sisters say?" My handle was getting stiff.

"They're married, too. But what do they care? My one sister said, 'The more the merrier.' Can you beat that? And her husband's a loser. He doesn't care. Nobody believes in anything anymore, I say. It's a wonder there's still one normal person like me left." She stared and pulled. Her fist seemed to hold an endless supply of quarters.

I patted my little machine and pulled the lever. Bells rang.

"Fruit salad!" the woman cried. "You got it, honey."

A red light flashed on top of my machine and quarters began spilling into the big metal cup. "How much did I win?" I asked, staring down at the flowing change.

"Only a fifty," the woman said, her voice dropping. She bit her lower lip and put one dagger-nailed finger to her scalp to scratch among the teased, jet-black curls. "You know, when I set myself here, I spent a few quarters in your machine there to try it out, then I picked this one. The machine's next to mine and I let you sit at it, and that's usually bad luck. I did you a favor. How about it?"

I began scooping the money into my pockets, into the paper cup left on top of the machine. I saw Cecil and Billy a few rows down. "Hey!" I called. Billy waved his cigarette. The woman pulled on my arm.

"C'mon," she pleaded. "Be fair. Let me in on it."

"I'm going to have a baby, for God's sake," I snapped. "Play your own damn machine. Look, here comes my lawyer. Now you better watch it." Without saying a word, Cecil shouldered the woman aside and scooped up the rest of the coins.

"That woman was crazy!" I said, as we headed toward the parking lot.

"Every time I leave you alone for a minute something happens," Billy said.

"I thought I got lucky."

"Stick with me and you'll really be rich. My woman." Billy ran his finger down my arm. "What a woman. What'll we do with the money?"

"Gamble some more," I said. "Let's go to that place with the waving cowboy sign, Cecil. How did you guys do?"

"I lost it all, hon," Billy said.

"Even with my expert advice," Cecil said. "Unimaginable."
He shook his head.

We all piled into the front seat of the Lincoln.

"Suffer," Billy said. "You make me suffer, woman. You're a gambling addict." He looked like he was going to cry.

"You're crazy, Billy. You're both crazy if you don't want to go somewhere else." I drained the drink Cecil had swiped from the bar. I felt heated, confident.

"Let's get my baby a gift," Billy said. He plastered my cheek with kisses.

"What kind of gift?" I asked, pushing him away.

"Cecil and I have been talking, sweetheart. He thinks it would be much better if we were married."

"What would be better? Will you move over, please? It's hot. Cecil, turn on the air conditioner."

"Yes, ma'am," Cecil said, laughing. He didn't move.

"The money would be better, Trace. More security, you know. A better risk."

"Money's got nothing to do with marriage, dope. Now let's hear more about this gift." I saw the parking lot attendant standing like a sentry out on the sidewalk, watching us in Cecil's car.

"What about the baby?" Cecil asked. He blew smoke at the side mirror. "You're going to provide that child with a solid home, I hope." He laughed. "I can get you a nice wedding ring for fifty," he added.

"Oh, come on," I said. "Baby-schmaby." We all laughed.

Wanda stuck her head in the car window. "Hi! I'm off and out of there. Whew! One more paw on my backside and I'd have pulled out my pistol."

"You carry a gun?" Billy asked. He gaped at Wanda, who was applying lipstick in the side mirror. She kissed at Billy.

"Get in the back," Cecil said. "We're going to Smitty's."

"Oooo," Wanda said. "Who's getting married?"

"What did these guys do to you?" Billy asked, as he climbed over the seat to get next to Wanda. "Cecil and I'll get 'em."

Cecil started the Lincoln and we glided out of the lot. I played with the electric window and tilted the air conditioner vent down into my lap. The rush of hot, dry air on my cheek and the cold on my legs were exquisite. Puffs of cool air surrounded my thighs, like huge hands grasping and then letting go. I looked at Cecil for a long minute. "I don't want to get married," I said.

"Nobody does," Cecil responded. "It's just that the time comes up and it seems the thing to do. It's sort of like deciding to go to the movies one night except you plan way in advance and pick an Academy Award winner. Sometimes there are extenuating circumstances."

"Yeah," I said dully. My head suddenly felt very heavy and grainy, my eyes rather weepy. The dashboard clock said 1:42 A.M. I saw Wanda and Billy's heads reflected in the rearview mirror. Then I thought I saw Wanda grit her teeth, grab a handful of Billy's hair, and pull his head roughly down into her lap.

"Ow! Jeez!" Billy laughed hysterically. "Show me your gun, Wanda," he said.

One had to be quick in this city, and aware, before too many things just started happening. I would be more on guard from now on, I decided, as I gently smashed my face against the side window of the car.

Wanda giggled. "Show me *your* gun, buckaroo," she whispered. I could hear them struggling.

Wanda squealed and kicked the back of the front seat as we turned into Smitty's. On the road an orange neon sign blinked the name of the place, but no light came from the building, which looked like a large hunting lodge.

Cecil got out of the car, followed by Billy, Wanda, and me. The front door opened into a cavernous room, filled with furniture. A deer head, a moose head, and old photographs of noble-looking Indians covered the walls. A red plaid jacket and a baseball cap hung from deer hooves mounted on a board. The only light in the room came from a long bar against the back wall, where a heavy, balding man wearing a string tie sat on a stool. He seemed totally unaffected by our entrance. I lurched drunkenly into a stereo cabinet as we made our way to the bar.

"Smitty has some rings to show you," Cecil said.

He made drinks at the bar while Smitty brought over a shoe box and emptied the contents on a piece of red felt.

I had never seen so many diamonds. There were fat, sparkly necklaces and bracelets and cocktail rings and a poodle pin shaped out of tiny diamonds. The eye was missing. I pinned it on my tank top while Billy looked at the rings. "These cost more than fifty bucks, Cecil," he said.

Smitty finally spoke: "As friends to my counselor here, you are entitled to a substantial discount. Besides, I like to see people get a good start in life, something I was not privy to."

"Awww, Smitty," Wanda said. "You're an okay guy by us."

"Yeah, now I am," he muttered.

Billy pretended to bite down on a necklace. Everyone laughed.

"I love this one," I said, picking out a gaudy diamond starburst. My finger exploded with light when I put it on. I jiggled the ring. "The woman who owned it must have been a linebacker," I said.

"Fifty dollars," Smitty said. "Firm."

"You like it, Tracy?" Billy asked.

I held the ring up to the track lights over the bar. It twinkled like all the signs on the Strip. "I'll take it," I said.

"Now we're engaged!" Billy cried, rushing to hug me.

"Forget it, buddy," I said, laughing, not taking my eyes off the ring. "This is just a bunch of diamonds."

"I think Tracy lacks a sense of the deep symbolism of material objects," Cecil said. Suddenly he stood in front of me, leering, it seemed. He handed me another drink.

"Just think," Wanda said, rapturous, "flowers, food, a beautiful ceremony, a long white gown. The handsome man you love by your side. Ahh."

"What is it with you guys?" I asked. "We don't have to get married to have a happy life. Right, Billy?"

"Of course not," Billy said. He grinned. "C'mon, Tracy, it'll be fun. Why not?"

"I can't believe your disrespect and ingratitude," Cecil said, grabbing my arm. He twisted his hand tight against my skin, smiling the whole time. "After this nice ring your boyfriend gave you and this money coming your way. We ask for a simple concession. You've. Got. To. Learn. Modesty." He shook me by the arm, yelling and laughing in my face.

I cringed against the bar. Cecil was a strong man. "Asshole!" I yelled, hitting his chest with my fist.

"Get your shit together, honey," Billy said, laughing.

"I think you and Tracy and I better have a talk," Cecil said. "In my office." He took my arm and hauled me out of Smitty's. Cecil pushed me into the front seat of the Lincoln and then climbed in next to me, while Billy sprawled across the back seat, his big feet hanging out the door.

Cecil opened all the windows and the sunroof, then reached under the seat and pulled out a bottle. He passed it to me. He shifted his huge body in the seat and coughed.

"You know, Tracy," Billy began, "it's not as if we've never touched on this topic before. I mean, I love you, you know that. Do you remember that time we went to the beach and we both said we could see ourselves walking on the same sand with each other forever?"

I felt weepy and hot, my mouth sour. My ring looked dull and clunky in the dark. Billy went on and on with a story I didn't remember.

"No, no," Cecil said, talking over Billy. "Baby or no baby, you look fine. You've probably just filled out. You know, rounded. Ripe." Cecil laughed and looked me over.

I took another drink from the bottle and closed my eyes. Everything outside the car, as if it were only in my imagination, just melted away. Billy was still talking. "All that money," I heard him say. "It would all be for us. Cars, boats, a house, no work, diamonds, dope . . ." And then Cecil started talking again, but I couldn't quite hear him. I thought he said: "Hand over hand, men and women go through life together. Of course. They work as a team, men and women. The great coupling. Sex is the glue, thick and satisfying. Don't you agree?"

I thought I felt Cecil's hand on my thigh, but when I looked down, he just had it resting on the seat between us. He wore a pinkie ring of diamonds shaped into his initials. I squeezed my fingers together. Our rings were not identical, but at least together they put out some sparkle in the dark.

". . . marriage a ritual, one ritual among many, what's the difference?" Cecil said. "Arms around waists, rings on fingers; circle your wagons, everyone. I believe in all the major social institutions," the voice next to me said. It laughed, long and loud.

My eyes kept snapping open and then slowly closing again. Smitty's sign spun and twirled like circus lights and its movement blended into Billy's song from the back seat: "I Only Have Eyes For You." "Oh, baby, let's just do it!" he suddenly cried.

Cecil leaned over me, brushing against my breast as he moved, and opened the glove compartment. I saw a pair of handcuffs resting on top of the Lincoln owner's manual. Cecil inserted the liquor bottle, its liquid sloshing, and closed the compartment door.

"Oh, Jesus," I whispered. Cecil grabbed my wrist and held it while I opened the car door and leaned out, vomiting neatly onto the ground. He pulled me up again.

"Just a little case of nerves," Cecil said, sliding a piece of chewing gum between my teeth. Billy laughed at his own private joke, cackling and snorting as if he were the funniest person alive.

"Come along, William," Cecil said, getting out of the car. "We have a lot to celebrate." I watched Cecil come around the front of the car, his body rolling across the desert toward me. I let him open my door, let him take my hand and lift me out. The three of us went back inside Smitty's.

"Oh! Oh! Here they are!" Wanda exclaimed as we came in. "Everyone ready?"

Cecil pulled me to the bar and sat me on a barstool. Billy sat down next to me.

"Take his hand, honey bun," Cecil said, grabbing my wrist and slapping my palm down on the bar.

"My sweetheart," Billy said, holding my fingers.

Smitty pulled a bottle of champagne and five glasses from behind the bar and once Cecil popped the cork, I was gone, slaloming in and out of the party for what seemed like hours. At one point I held a silk rose while Billy spun my new ring around my finger and everyone cheered. "I do!" I yelled, then drifted out again.

Cecil, Wanda, and Billy looked like cardboard figures under the bar lights, stiff and one-dimensional, with flat, staring eyes. For a while, Cecil was behind me, his breath on my neck like a strong wind; then he was beside me feeling my hair between his fingers as if it were a fine material. Later, I saw Wanda slide her arms around Billy's waist and lift him off the ground. He howled.

Finally, I heard Wanda say: "Tracy honey's tired."

"Ohhh, Tracy honey." That was Billy.

"This is no attitude to take toward such an important night," Cecil said.

"Or in my place," Smitty said.

"We all need some air," Cecil continued. "Where shall we go?"

"The Strip," I muttered. I had my head on the bar.

"I think we should pay our respects to my Uncle Hector and his junk shop. He's the man who made all this possible." Billy hit the bar. "Let's go."

We tore down the highway, then turned and turned again.

"Are we going in a circle?" I asked Cecil. The car screeched onto a dirt road. Animals ran outside the range of our headlights. Las Vegas sat in a radioactive glow on the horizon.

Hector's store was a ghost-town building sitting all alone in the scrub, sagging at one end and flanked by huge barrel and organ pipe cacti. Black seemed to glow out from its windows.

Cecil unlocked the front door and stepped back, then Billy creaked it open and flipped a switch.

Inside, Cecil propped me up against a china cabinet, which leaned against an endless row of other run-down furniture. Cheap tapestries hung limply from the ceiling; I could see one of Elvis and one of horses and leprechauns in a glade. Old lamps covered a long counter before me—ugly ones with fringe shades and plastic crystal drops. Dozens of toasters and broken-down Veg-o-Matics crowded a shelf behind the counter.

"Billy, and now Tracy," Cecil said, "this whole place is yours."

Billy looked over at me. "Picture a house on a hill, roses climbing a fence," he began.

"Shut up," I muttered.

"Now, an assessment," Cecil said. "Just peruse the place and make a mental note of valuables. You and Wanda go that way and Tracy and I will cover this wing."

Billy and Wanda drifted off behind a bank of old jukeboxes. Cecil led me under the moving tapestries; we were royalty in a crumbling kingdom.

Cecil held my right bicep firmly. Every few seconds his fingers sunk a bit deeper into my muscle, then let go. We wandered among card tables and old washing machines and Singer treadles. I felt as if Cecil and I were shopping for a home appliance, only nothing looked good.

"I'll show you something you can't get rid of," Cecil finally said.

We passed a table covered with hood ornaments and came

to a huge room, a separate addition to the building, filled with ornately carved four-poster beds. "Did a fancy bordello have a closeout?" I asked.

"These were Hector's pride and joys."

"And we're to keep them all?" I collapsed on a bed and bounced a few times. I felt sick. A tapestry of peacocks displaying their tails in front of the Manhattan skyline waved over my head.

Cecil sat down on the bed next to mine and lit a cigarette. He offered me a sip from his cup, but I just covered my mouth. He drank deep, smoked his cigarette down, and then asked: "How's the new heiress? You and Billy may want to consult with me on possible investments."

I closed my eyes in reply. I reached for Cecil's cup and he gave it to me, smiling. "Don't you ever get tired of giving advice?" I asked. I took a long drink.

Cecil got up and moved to my bed. "The lawyer-client relationship is sacred," he whispered. "Complicated and intimate."

Cecil looked as fresh as when he had picked up Billy and me, which seemed like days ago. The gentle crow's-feet around his eyes crinkled as he smiled down at me. Not a warm smile, or a suggestive one, just wise.

Cecil kissed me hard and sure, no funny business, no love. It wasn't as if he were cruel or cold, it was as if a deal had already gone through. This movement was part of the aftermath. The cleaning up.

I kept my eyes focused on the tapestries and the crummy ceiling while Cecil slowly moved his hand down my arm. I heard voices at the entrance to the room. Billy and Wanda stood in the doorway with their arms around each other. Wanda broke into giggles and Billy said sternly, "Let's go. It's time to go." But a smile played around the corners of his mouth.

The Money Stays, the People Go

I woke to hear the motel room door slam against its chain and someone mutter in Spanish. "Maid," the voice outside said. She pushed against the door a few more times, rattling the chain, then closed it and left.

The windows were covered with blackout curtains; the air conditioner roared. I could see Billy and Wanda entwined on the other double bed. Billy snored, Wanda lay with her mouth open, her small teeth bright in the dark. On the bedside table sat her crumpled, frosty wig.

I didn't need to turn over but I did. There was Cecil, flat on his back, not a hair out of place. I had discovered that his beautiful tan ran everywhere, except for narrow wedge shapes around his private areas. The man harbored no inconsistencies and held no surprises, just steely determination against all odds—a characteristic I aspired to have, a characteristic I could learn from. I had given in this time, but that was it—never again. I would be like Cecil, a piece of ice in the Nevada desert—impossible, persistent.

I leaned over Cecil's perfect face.

"It's all taken care of," he said.

I hesitated for a second, then kept on going down.

Occidental

After a game of darts and a couple of rounds, Bob Olmstad slammed out of Dick's Tavern and into the waning light. He rocked on his heels, trying to get his equilibrium, while he scoped out the strangers in town. Two kids, a boy and a girl in their early twenties, Bob guessed, loitered in the undefined, blasted space that marked the center of the village, looking as bored and weary as if they'd already done hard time in the world. More important, Bob thought, tucking in his shirt, they looked like they deserved a visit. He took off, veering unsteadily through the fifty yards of no-man's land that separated him from the kids, the neck of a new bottle of Wild Turkey, a gift from the bar, garroted in his right hand.

Bob stopped, looked down upon the young couple, and cracked open his bottle. He was on a five-day drunk to facilitate grieving for his mother, but he wondered, as the boy and girl blinked up at him and drew in toward each other, at the shift in direction his sadness had suddenly taken. These two kids, with their blank faces, their tabulae rasae, seemed to fuel his misery somehow, threatened to drag him down further to a layer of shrouded memories he'd rather not uncover. He gave a limp salute and sat down.

"Welcome to paradise," Bob said, gesturing toward their surroundings. Just a concrete square, an old building foundation that sat like an abandoned helicopter pad in a jungle of weeds, sage, and horsetail, a clutter of old beer cans, and a sweat sock or two—it was hardly auspicious, but it was, at that moment, the new Margaret Olmstad Memorial Park of Occidental, California. Bob, Occidental's own holy man, had only to stride upon the ground, conjure up an image of his mother, now a week deceased, and create this blessed spot. Abracadabra.

The boy, a college kid, he figured, relaxed and lit a cigarette. "This is paradise?" the kid said, laughing and blowing out smoke. "*Fin de siècle* paradise," he added quietly, a joke to himself.

"Yeah, yeah, paradise in decline," Bob said, laughing. "I'm not as dumb as I look."

The girl laughed, too, a tinkling giggle. Bob smiled hard at her. She had that blurred look some young women had, their features still settling. But the guy, he was a type: Bob could see him in a Berkeley cafe flipping through fat, unreadable books and smoking fancy brown cigarettes, a grown-up baby. Yeah, why not, Bob thought, still smiling, I'll mourn him, too. Both of them.

"As a matter of fact," Bob said, "I'm the mayor of this paradise. Hizzoner of Occidental. Bob Olmstad."

"Come on," the kid said. "You're drunk."

"This is true," Bob said. "But drunk and mayor are not mutually exclusive."

"I believe him, Jason," the girl said urgently. "Look at his eyes."

Bob winced. Don't, oh, don't look there, he thought.

*

When Bob had met his eyes that very morning in the mirror at Myra's house, he'd almost gasped. They were so cracked and red and shot through with seeping grief that when he slipped on his little gold spectacles, the red stains on his eyes seemed to crawl across his lenses too, shattering the glass. And the rest of him: none too good with his blond-to-gray hair awry, some strands stuck up like broom straws, his scrawny red neck exposed and blotchy face slack. But when he'd jumped back in bed to try to wake Myra by giving her a sip from his bottle, that's when she threw him out. "Go kill yourself someplace else!" she had yelled, tossing his clothes after him onto the gravel driveway in her fury of swooshing caftan.

Bob knew exactly what Myra was up to right now. Finished with some godawful micro-macro dinner, she was doing yoga, or tai chi, ringing gongs, meditating, chanting the sacred word. Bob often sat nearby during these performances, smoking, reading magazines, appreciating her efforts. He admired her finely lined face puckered in concentration while she moved, her long brown hair run through with gray swinging below her shoulders. Her full woman's body looked good even in an old sweat suit. Adorned with long bead earrings, the four silver rings she never removed, and an army of clacking stone necklaces, Myra would do a kind of dance to welcome another spirit's presence, strike a pose like a fish, a camel, whatever, or simply sit quietly, her eyes looking inside, she said, all the while laboring to become something or someone else. Whatever she did she did like her life depended on it, which was just as well considering she was set up for eternity and didn't have to work. Old hippie money, she said. She had a searcher's luxury.

"Yes, this place is all mine," Bob said aloud to the kids, startling himself back to the town square. The kids, convinced, perhaps, or nervous, gazed along the single street of small shops circling the center, most of them closed up for the evening. Useless places. You could find hundred-dollar roller skates, bags of fava beans, and brass door knockers shaped like sunflowers, but, aside from drinks at the tavern, you couldn't buy any merchandise in town that a real person would want. No penny nails, no nylons, not even a package of Twinkies. Instead you got all that stylish clutter, that transplanted hip, facing this blank spot, a monument to swift obsolescence.

Bob gestured broadly toward the hills of pines and redwoods behind the shops that squeezed the village into a narrow valley. A vulnerable place, open to ambush. Most people lived in the hills, or out on the winding road to Bodega Bay. "I've heard there's some real live Druids living outside town," Bob whispered, leaning forward. He knew he would find even Druids indistinguishable from the town's other yuppies—the boutique owners, lawyers, and woodchucks, all the other seekers, their BMWs and stock portfolios equally well cared for.

"Now your Druids per se are an extinct people," Bob continued solemnly, plucking a cigarette from Jason's pack. "As we all will be some day," he added. "*Fin de siècle.*"

"Well, sure," Jason said, stretching, "when the sun moves toward the earth and we all burn up."

"I mean now, laddie," Bob said. "Can't you smell the smoke?" He winked.

The girl shivered. She still had a child's face, round with baby fat, but a woman's bones in the jaw and wrists. Her skin wore a sheet of freckles. Where did she fit in? An old flame from the home town? The kid couldn't get anyone else to listen to him? And she was pretty, too, in a neighbor-girl kind of way, with long red hair in that new style of crimped tendrils; her head looked like an orange Boston fern. Bob's mother, Margaret, had raised one of those, in the "front room," as they called the living room in the kind of Chicago bungalow Bob grew up in. She was so proud of it, spraying water on it every day from a gold can. The fern grew forever, all through Bob's childhood, outliving pets, neighbors, almost his mother herself.

The girl turned her lively face to Bob. "It doesn't help to worry about such things, like the world ending," she said. "It's good to remember that."

"I see." Bob suppressed a laugh. Hell, worry was fuel. Worry was what told people his mother's age that they were alive. Worry was what he and Myra and all the rest their age were trying to transform. Into what? Pleasure? Oblivion? And these kids? Look away from worry, they said, throw it to the bottom of a black hole. He marveled at the couple's unmarked skin, flat and smooth as an embryo's hide. Newborns looked like little old men, as if they started out on the wrong end of time. The years passing were like that, slipping and lurching forward, sometimes leaving you behind. In the few days since his mother had died, Bob felt like he was flipping backward through a photo album, watching himself get smaller, his mother younger, until they were both just ideas, blips of life unimagined.

"Here's a story," Bob said a short time later, bringing the bottle to his lips.

Jason glanced at a nonexistent watch, then quickly up at the dimming sky. "Kim and I have to go," he said. "We have to get to Mendocino."

"You can't leave town without a story," Bob said. He suddenly felt desperate to keep these snotnoses around. If they left, it'd just be him and, what? Old Margaret's crabby ghost? "You want to gather material, don't you?" he asked them. "How often do you meet a real live colorful character?" He threw out his arms.

"Yeah," Kim said, laughing, sitting up in anticipation. "We have time for a story. Don't we, Jason?"

"Okay, okay," Jason said, leaning back on his elbows. "Just a short one." He rolled his eyes at the pines and redwoods. Bob slowly spread his hands out in the air. "Silence, children," he whispered. Diversionary tactics. He had no idea what he was going to say, but it had to be something big to keep them there. Something they couldn't top in their own lives no matter how long they lived. He closed his eyes. "This tale takes place long ago," Bob began, "in an ancient land called Vietnam."

Jason let out a deep sigh and fell back onto the ground.

"My uncle went," Kim said eagerly. "To the war."

"A bad time," Bob said quietly, his eyes still closed. He tried to will himself back, to repair this scraggly narrative he had started, to change direction. Where was he going with this story? Nowhere safe.

"A bad time," Bob said again, "but then you all know that. You've seen the movies, haven't you?" he asked. He stopped. "Well, haven't you?" He almost shouted.

"Sure." Jason's voice rose dully from the ground.

Eyes closed again, spooling out the past as carefully as if it were razor wire. "Our platoon was ordered to search and clear out this hamlet, scare up any VC," Bob began.

"Search and destroy," Jason said from the ground. "So what else is new?"

Bob paused. He had told this story before, to his mother, when he returned home, when she asked, pleaded with him to say *something*. It was two stories really, connected, marking one of the few times during the war when there did seem to be a link between events, a moral to the tale. But if he was going to go on, he'd have to skip some parts of the story for these TV-heads. Get to the juice, the meat, the violence—that's what they understood. Pump the gore. And for God's sake, leave out the mind-pulverizing boredom that always precipitated the killing. Like the quiet, the dead sound, the insects and birds ominously still, before the carpet bombers flew over on a mission.

"Okay," Bob continued, "so we drag out these families, out into the open. We're down in the well, under the shacks, digging up gardens, rounding them all up. Nothing there, really, but we've got to do something. Burn it down and move the people. And then go and do it again down the way. That old army cycle of futility shit." He stopped for a second, breathed. "Anyway, they load up. They've got everything on their backs or on the oxcarts, little pigs on rope leashes, rice pots, the whole bit. One of the last ones to go is this ancient guy, tiny and skinny, with Ho Chi Minh whiskers and gray pj's. He turns to this buddy of mine, our platoon leader, and he says something to him, quiet, like he really means it."

"What'd he say?" Kim asked, her eyes wide.

"Damned if I know," Bob said, breaking out into a laugh that soon became a wheezy cough. Kim and Jason exchanged looks. Don't stop now, Bob thought. Get to the point. Right, even these kids want a center to this.

"But I found out later from my buddy, our platoon leader," Bob said. "What the old man said. It was a few nights later and my buddy and I were enjoying some choice weed, experimenting on that temporal plain." Bob stopped. "Did you know that time moves different in the more ancient cultures? Minutes move slower. Did you know some cultures have no sense of time at all? Some even have no past or future tenses in their language. No words for time as we know it. It's a proven fact." He stopped again. What were those guys called? Sappers. A lieutenant once told him about these Vietcong who came screaming and running into bunkers with loads of explosives tied to their backs. What do they care? the lieutenant said. They think they're coming back again. And the next time will be better.

"Well, folks," Bob continued, "my buddy—let's give him a name, why don't we? Lycomb, my buddy, our platoon leader, he passed me the joint." Bob demonstrated, clenching his breath. "And I can remember this so well, it was so dark I couldn't really see his face, just heard his voice come out of the black at me." Bob exhaled. "So Lycomb says, 'The old way is gone, the new way uncertain.'" Bob looked at the couple. "That's what gramps said."

Jason burst out laughing; Kim hit him on the arm and tried to shush him. "Oh, come on," Jason said, sputtering, then he was off again laughing.

"I sense your disbelief," Bob said. He hiccupped.

Jason said, "How about: 'Get your fat ass off my land, Yankee'? Or: 'Die, capitalist pig'? 'The old way is gone,' *please*."

"Okay, okay, so I can't verify it. But Lycomb said it and, after all, what's the difference? Either way the old goat was telling us to go to the moon. Us and all our detritus. There was nothing waiting for us at the end."

There was silence for a minute. The low-lying sunshine broke through some pines and struck Bob's face. He could feel the dissipating heat work around his neck: a visitation, a warm touch, like someone waking him up. He raised his shoulder to wipe sweat from his temple, he waved away a fly. Kim stared at him.

"You got wounded, didn't you?" she asked suddenly.

"Kim!" Jason glared at her.

Bob laughed. "Oh, he's worried I might have got my balls shot off, and that's how come I'm sittin' here, the mayor, drunk on a weeknight," he said to Kim. He shook his finger at her. "I knew you'd seen those movies. All that sobbing veteran shit. Makes the audience feel better, don't it?" Bob took a swallow of Wild Turkey. "An injury like that? No, actually, I have my very own lady friend, who seems happy enough. At intervals." Myra always said: Working on myself is working on us. In that case, Bob thought with brief clarity, your own happiness was only a matter of someone else surviving.

"This story ain't finished," Bob said, noticing Jason's impatience. "Don't you want to hear the punch line?"

"Sure. Go ahead," Jason said. He lay back on the concrete. Kim looked at him and then looked away.

"Another thing Lycomb told me that night," Bob continued. "He said we were going to pay for our deeds. It was going to get us back."

"'It'?" Kim asked. "What?"

"Well, that's when Lycomb started telling me about the Angel Girl. Until he was rudely interrupted."

"Like a real angel?" Kim asked.

"No, sugar, a Vietnamese angel," Bob said.

"They don't believe in angels," Jason said. "They're Buddhists."

"Lycomb was mistaken, you see," Bob said, ignoring him. "He had it all wrong. He was trying to explain karma, but he got it mixed up with some love slop some girl he met on leave tried to tell him. Personally, I think it was the weed talking." The sun had fallen behind the far hills, its light sinking into a pool of shadows. Soon the stars would be out.

"Lycomb's idea," Bob continued, "was that the Angel Girl brings back every bomb you drop, all the bullets fired, flies east with them—you know, back here," he slapped the ground, "and gives them back to the perpetrators. Bam, bam, one for one."

"Right," Jason said. "Karma."

"Lycomb's version of karma," Bob said. He stopped, took a swallow. This was the part he could mess up. It was like telling somebody about a film: You had to run the scenes through your head while you narrated, and in doing that you lost part of the experience—how you felt about the movie the first time you saw it, what made it worth remembering, the whole damn point. The children waited uneasily, restless on the buckled cement.

How you felt about anything the first time, Bob thought, drifting through his memory. Margaret was at the end of everything he could recount, the first and last voice he heard, no matter how hard he resisted her.

When Bob came home from his first tour that spring, moving between periods of dead sleep and fist fights, his mother just watched him for a while. Who was *she*? he thought at the time. Only a Chicago widow in her housecoat running roughshod with a dust rag and a mop. He started drinking, drank so much she wouldn't let him in one night but left him on the front stoop, the yellow porch light burning into his cracked-open eyes. All night, the same parade of pictures: Those Vietnamese girls wading through the rice paddies, starting to run at the sight of the soldiers, braids down their backs swinging, temple roof hats bobbing. *The self is a sanctuary, a holy place.* Myra said that, read that. And the grunts following the girls through the rice, crouching, harvesting with guns.

His mother appeared early the next morning, put her hands on her hips for a minute, then propped open the screen door with her foot and spoke to Bob as if she were addressing an annoying salesman.

"So you think you messed up, so what?" Margaret said, her Norwegian accent strengthened by anger. "We all make our own worlds, Robert, little ones for ourselves where we try to set things right. That's the best you can do and, cripes, just live with it all unfinished. Now come on in here."

Kim and Jason's faces seemed to illuminate suddenly, but then Bob realized it was the flame from his lighter, weaving toward a cigarette he held between his teeth. It was time to fire up this memory.

"Lycomb wasn't right about karma," Bob said, resuming, "but he was about other matters. Later that night everyone was asleep, or supposed to be, and Lycomb and I were on watch, keeping each other awake. We're talking, we're sharing the weed. Then, while we're laughing at one of Lycomb's stupid-ass jokes, I see the air go white. One second I'm looking at Lycomb's jaws open in a grin, and then the shell hits, too close, so the next second he's lit up so bright I can sort of see through his skin. Like he's just made of paper, transparent. Fuckin' A, that first shell! And after that everybody in the platoon's up and running, just trying to get the hell out of there."

"Oh, God," Kim said. She and the punk were turning a kind of putty color in the gloom; they looked waxy, lifeless.

"I stayed with Lycomb while he got on the radio, fast," Bob said, trying to breathe steadily. "Turned out the only other unit in our area was us."

"'Us'?" Kim asked. "Who?"

"Our illustrious troops, honey," Bob said. "That's who was lobbing the shells."

"It's called friendly fire," Jason said, sitting up to light a cigarette. His lowered eyelids looked as smooth as drawn window shades.

"It's called Lycomb karma, poor bastard," Bob said. He paused and looked past his audience. All the shops were dark, their windows staring out, just dim lights in the back rooms. Counting their money. Bob felt rather than saw the night descend over Occidental. It pulled his shoulders down, pulled out the next barrage of words.

"So Lycomb's on the radio," Bob said, still gazing past Jason and Kim, "and he's trying to get this unit on the horn, he's screaming, the shells are screaming, the rest of the platoon is running. I see a couple of guys go down. I remember Lycomb hitting the ground flat with the radio receiver, just yelling. I've got my rifle and I'm trying to cover him, for what it's worth, I don't know. Finally he starts this, what do you call it?" Bob giggled and wiped his face with his hand. "Mantra? Whatever. Okay, so he starts this mantra on the radio: 'What the fuck! Over,' he says. Repeats it. 'What the fuck! Over. What the fuck-over.' Each time a bomb comes in. 'Lycomb,' I'm yelling

—'we've got to move, man!' 'What the fuck-over!' Lycomb's only a few yards away, mind you, and I'm there, I'm covering him. 'Over! Over!' he's yelling. 'Fuck! Over!' Then this big arc of light. I have time to watch it come, it's so goddamn slow. And as I watch the shell go one way, I start to scramble the other way. Away! Away! You see, I'm moving away from Lycomb with my rifle, but what am I covering? Nothin' now but me. Then the flash. It's that Angel Girl. Coming at ya, Lycomb. And there he went. Snatched away. No more Lycomb as we know him."

Bob lifted the bottle to his lips. His hands were shaking. There we go, he thought. Dead center. Dead silence.

Kim looked away, smoothing her jeans hard over her thighs. Jason examined Bob. What was that look? Bob thought. Emptiness? Christ, was it pity? Coming back at ya, kid.

"We gotta go," Jason said suddenly. He stood up and held out his hand to Kim. She refused it and took her time getting up, hooking her leather backpack over both shoulders.

Bob coughed, stretched out uneasily on his elbows, tried to smile. "As the one and only member of the Occidental Traveler's Aid, I wish you a safe journey," he said. "And come back again." From the ground he shook hands with Jason. The boy turned his back on him and lit a cigarette, already looking down the road. Kim bent down and kissed Bob's cheek.

Bob lay back on the concrete after he heard their car start up and roar away. What a sight he must be to all his constituents! Their mayor flat out on the ground with a snootful, crying a dry cry.

And what was that ancient story supposed to mean? Unearthed, inspected, now preserved like a mummy; the dead not quite dead. All Bob knew was that he couldn't really do anything—then, as a lowly grunt, or now, in his august office of mayor. The days didn't move along as they had when his mother was young—forward, with purpose. Now you let your life twist in the breeze and you smiled away as if you were really on firm ground. Sometimes you were given a semblance of responsibility to carry with you, like a town, your own platoon of sorts. All those Druids, account executives, computer programmers, babies—they were all Bob's to protect, plus land, sky, trees, groundwater, this park. Margaret Olmstad Memorial Park was dark now, the concrete cold. Gotta get some lights in here, Bob thought. A bench. Grass.

He heard the rattle of Myra's old diesel Mercedes long before he turned his head and caught sight of it moving under a street lamp down the block. Myra bumped the car over the low curb, onto the weeds, crept over to the concrete. He'd have to get a fence. A fountain. Flowers of the season. The old is reborn, better than before. The passenger side door of Myra's car opened with a creak, the scent of sandalwood oil and joss sticks escaping into the cool air.

"All right, Robert," Myra said. She paused, then slapped the seat beside her. "Come on, sweetheart. All is forgiven. I've got a place here for my baby boy." She waited again. "Jesus, man, are you all right?" she asked.

Bob didn't answer. Instead he watched as stars punched through the blackening sky, each a huge continuous explosion so far away it had expired by the time its light reached earth. His mother had told him that every time a person died, a new star came into being. Which one was Ma? Bob squinted at the sky. Which one was poor Lycomb? And which star was promised for these vast millions surrounding him, still waiting to be born?

Disaster

One July weekend in Chicago, twenty-four people were murdered. The exact number appeared on the TV screen the following Monday night under the face of the most recent victim, an elderly black man. I was eight years old and up past my bedtime. We were deep into hot weather, but I was able to watch the news reports while huddled in a blanket because it was during this summer that my parents had had a financial windfall, bought central air conditioning, and closed up the house.

The murders confirmed what I'd been told all along. Danger was everywhere outside; it wasn't safe to open the door or talk to anyone new. Even fresh air was suspect. My parents told me stories of children kidnapped on the way home from school; of fast cars; of false friends who lied and stole toys; of branches that fell from trees without warning. I took their word for it and ran straight home from school every day. In class I remained stubbornly quiet so nothing I said could be used against me.

Outside my house I imagined a limitless space filled with random terror, accidents, and the screams of millions of strangers. Closer to home things seemed more manageable, available to touch and smell—like leaves, and the persistent stench of the fungus on the maple trees in my front yard. The things I liked best were closest at hand: my toys, my furniture, the television set.

That Monday night, the dead man's face hung on the television screen, smiling and innocent, oblivious to fate. I learned that these murders were part of a trend. Just two weeks earlier a schoolteacher in my suburb had been stabbed. The murderer had shoved his knife right through her screen door. The schoolteacher had thought he was selling something.

After the teacher was stabbed, my mother said, "I can see it now. Kids will be drawing pictures in school of bloody teachers. Children are always drawing pictures of what they are really afraid of. You just keep drawing trees, Lindy, like you usually do, so I don't have to put up pictures of bloody teachers on the refrigerator."

My mother put her hand on my forehead and pushed up my bangs, smearing them back over the top of my head. I had secretly cut my hair one day while hiding behind the big living-room chair and now I looked rakish. My mother insisted I had to suffer for my silliness. She refused to take me to my regular barber shop, where I was the only little girl among hair tonic ads and men with cigars. I now suffered with my mother's hand on me. She smelled of cigarettes.

After the murders I gave up the trees and drew mug shots instead, using men and women from the news and game shows as my models. I also drew the faces I had seen on the "Most Wanted" lists at the post office, where I went every Saturday with my father. Only on these trips was I not afraid, but excited. I made a point of watching the men we passed on the street in case they might be criminals. The idea of catching a crook was invigorating: I would yell "That's him!" and my father would rush me off to the police station for a statement under his arm, my eyes agog. I especially liked the idea of my face in the paper—a crook catcher—wearing that expectant look I always saved for rare moments of self-confidence. I drew the mug shots in the classic front and profile manner, two drawings side by side, and tacked them to my bedroom wall.

"Where are your nice tree pictures?" my mother asked a few days after the murders. She peered at my drawing of the twenty-fourth victim. "Now who is this man?"

"He was on TV last night," I said.

"I don't recognize him from any show."

"He's dead."

"Oh. What was he famous for, do you know?"

"He was on TV."

That night I pulled the small television into the bathroom so I could watch the news while I took a bath. The city had quieted down after the killing weekend. Mayor Daley promised summer job programs for the poor, and a couple of kids drowned in Lake Michigan. While in the bathtub, I imagined Mayor Daley's mug shot, fat face forward and to the side.

"You'll electrocute yourself!" I heard my mother call through the locked door. Her knuckles sounded polite on the wood.

"I'm okay," I said.

"Dry off in the tub after you let the water out," my father said. Ice cubes clinked in his glass.

I was so close to danger, just a few feet away from zapping myself, from sending my crooked hair into ecstasy around my head. I splashed water on the TV but nothing happened.

"I heard that," my father called. "Keep your hands in the bathtub."

I turned back to the TV set. A golfer had been hit by lightning during a tournament. He was rolled away on a stretcher, his feet in cleats flapping to the sides as paramedics installed him in the ambulance.

"Come out of there now," my mother called. "We're having dinner. Be a good girl."

I closed my eyes and saw golf clubs, or lightning bolts, or something more hard and tangible and unbreakable shoot down on my parents. They went up in smoke outside the bathroom door.

My father, hoping with all his heart that I was technologically inclined, taught me to operate the stereo system in the living room. I sat on the living-room floor that summer with my elementary science book, listening to *The Best of the Ink Spots*. I read about infinity.

In my book, infinity was a one followed by a hundred zeroes. Dutifully, I counted them all. Scientists were not sure infinity was real, but they needed it to know the size of space. My father pointed to infinity when he showed me stars out the window. Infinity was as endless as Chicago and as stuffed with peril. My mother passed by the window as I looked up from my book; she wore a scarf and held a garden trowel. She traveled through infinity, weeding, going to the store, and still she avoided disaster. She waved and smiled.

The doorbell rang. When I opened the door I saw an orange-haired girl about my age standing stiffly on the other side of the glass storm door. She had a puffy and serious face loaded with freckles. I didn't know her from school.

"I live over there!" she screamed, waving her left arm down the block.

I craned my neck to see where she was pointing, but she seemed to be indicating our garage.

"I'm Margaret!" she screamed.

"Be more quiet!" I yelled back.

"We've got a pool!"

"Okay!" I screamed at the top of my lungs. Margaret looked surprised. I closed the heavy front door, then ran to the big picture window in the living room. Margaret walked by slowly, like an insulted Miss America, glaring at me through the glass. I ran from one room to the next, watching as she circled determinedly outside the house three times, the last time running at full speed. She fled from the front yard yelling, "I put a spell on you!"

I put a mug shot of Margaret up on my wall. Hers was the first drawing of a real person I knew. I wrote "Margaret" under her picture and drew a small blue heart next to her name. Under this I wrote "pool." The background of the drawing was strafed with a rainbow of curly lines; this, Margaret's home, I labeled "infinity."

"Well, at least you've got someone your own age up here," my father said. He peered at Margaret's picture, a drink in one hand, some papers from work in the other.

I was nervous about the heart on the drawing. Maybe it was too much. I concentrated on how the glass would feel in my father's hand, cold and slimy, and the weight of the papers, light and thin like a dead bird I had once held.

"That's a nice one," my mother said, as she entered my room. She smiled at me and patted my head. The moon-shaped streetlamp shone outside the window. My mother quickly snapped shut the curtains.

I worried over the next few weeks whether Margaret's spell meant trouble, and if I would survive it to live into old age. Perhaps she planned for my house to blow up, or a plane to crash into my backyard. I tested my stomach for queasiness, a sure sign of tragedy, but felt nothing. I decided that it was a friendly spell and hoped it would make my mother pregnant, or bring other good fortune.

Then, more worry. My parents told me they were going

away for the evening and a reliable next-door neighbor boy would stay with me. He was eighteen and had many friends who spit on the sidewalk and swore a lot. He mowed our lawn, occasionally turning his sour face to me, sitting safely inside. Alan, the boy, insisted on calling me "Kid."

"Please," I said, always polite, "call me Lindy." I was watching through the picture window while my parents drove out of sight.

Alan laughed and pulled my braids.

It was Saturday afternoon, so I switched on the TV to see if the lightning-struck golfer had returned to the tournament. He had, and he got rounds of applause at each hole he played. The natural phenomenon hadn't hurt him any; instead, he seemed more powerful than ever. The movement of his swing was like an eye snapping open.

I turned off the set and sat across from Alan at the kitchen table. He worked on math problems for summer school while I read about Venus's-flytraps in my science book. I imagined one of these plants in Margaret's garden, under another one of her spells, its mouth closing around my finger, gripping hard.

Alan made hamburgers for dinner. He ate three and I ate half of one, with a whole bun folded around it like a blanket. Alan had a huge head with an enormous mouth. I imagined gears clanking while he ate. Thick, straight hair, like grass, fell in his eyes.

By the time the after-dinner game shows came on, Alan was sipping his second beer, the phone receiver pressed to his ear. I understood that boys were coming over and only hoped they wouldn't spit in the house. I sat at the kitchen table. A mug shot of Alan lay to my right, drawn a week earlier from what I had seen of him through my window. I was now revising, making his head much larger.

Soon boys streamed through the front door. At Alan's request I had turned on the stereo, and I played the Ink Spots record until he told me to take it off. Then I found The Beatles on the radio and everyone seemed happy. More boys came.

"Kid," Alan said at one point, "let's have a party."

"Okay," I said, not looking up. We were all crammed in the living room where I worked furiously with my crayons and paper, drawing mug shots. Boys with big heads.

The music grew louder and everyone danced, spilling drinks and beer on the carpet. About a dozen boys flailed around the living room, trying out the Twist, tossing their crew-cut heads around in the hazy air. Alan sat smoking a cigarette and coughing, his eyes closed. I glanced around to get exact facial features for my drawings, but ignored the mess. My parents couldn't blame me as I would have been in bed.

At that moment, I looked out the picture window and saw an orange globe skim the tops of the shrubs. It was Margaret, spying. Her head looked a little like the drawing I had in my room of John Glenn's fiery spacecraft reentering the earth's atmosphere. Margaret's pale, dotted face rose over the bushes and scanned the living room. Her eyes fastened on me and she scowled, fiercely. She had escaped from her own home! I stared back, marveling at Margaret's bravery. Now she was a member of that flock of irresponsible children who glided by my house every day on foot, and on bikes and trikes, dodging tornadoes and train wrecks, looking under rocks and through mud for even more danger and chaos. I watched these kids through my bedroom window as if I were witness to a funeral march. Margaret's head retreated, the orange globe slid on. No good would come of her visitation, I was sure.

I wandered into the kitchen and nibbled some potato chips I found on the table. Alan was on the phone again with some boy beside him who kept trying to take the receiver away. Alan kissed into the phone. Now girls were coming over.

A softball whizzed by my head. The boy near the phone caught it and threw it back out of the room. He saw me, smiled, then picked me up and sat me on his shoulders. We jogged into the living room.

"Kid!" some of the boys shouted.

I smiled and waved, dizzy from the great height. The boy who held me was doing the Twist and I felt queasy every time he rotated down and up. When he stood straight my head grazed the ceiling.

A man delivered four pizzas to the house and Alan set them on the coffee table. He handed me up a piece with olives. I picked them off and dropped them in the boy's blond hair, which made a perfect launching pad: every time he gyrated up or down the olives spun out from his head. I was starting to have fun.

But then a fast song came on the stereo and the blond went wild. I had to duck to avoid getting a concussion; my braids were flying. Now my neck would surely be broken, as my parents had often predicted. I screamed at the top of my lungs.

The boy set me down. I dashed to the end of the hall, sat down, and cried, running my legs in frustration against the carpet. I imagined Margaret in my situation. She would have handled things differently: a cartoon swashbuckler in high boots, striding through the house, tossing boys aside and growling at them until they picked up all their mess. Instead, someone bounced a basketball in my room. A couple of boys wrestled in my parents' room. Two boys stood at the linen closet, looking down the laundry chute.

One of them turned and said, "Hey, Kid, where does this go?"

"Lindy!" I cried. I was exhausted. Boys danced in the living room, ate pizza, called girls on the phone. Sports were going on all over the house. Everyone called me "Kid."

"It goes to the basement," I said. The basement was where my father kept out-of-season things like my sled and skates and his shovels and the long pole with the metal half-moon that he used for breaking ice. These dangerous articles waited patiently for winter, like trolls under a bridge.

One of the boys threw his empty beer can down the chute. It clattered onto the basement floor. The other took off his T-shirt and threw it down. More boys from the living room wandered up to the closet, peered down the chute, and threw in their beer cans. Alan tossed the Ink Spots record. Soon everything was going down the laundry chute. Alan sent some of his friends to the basement to wait at the bottom. They tried to throw things back up. The boy I had danced with put me back on his shoulders and we joined the others. When I peered toward the end of the chute I was faced with a swirling darkness, and shouts coming from below. The softball came back up.

"Let's see if the Kid'll go down!" Alan yelled.

"Yeah!" all the other boys said.

Before I could scream, Alan took me off his friend's shoulders and pointed my head down into the laundry chute. I felt my shoulders go in and then the rest of me. Someone held my feet. Like a torpedo primed for firing, I started to shudder. All I could picture was an expanse of dark space and millions of stars, and my body shooting through it all. This was the stuff of my nightmares—the loneliest place in all infinity. I was up against exactly what I had been trying to avoid. I was sure my parents would be interviewed on the news after my disappearance, my mother crying, my father shaking his head and staring at his fingernails. Alan would get in big trouble for losing me. I screamed.

They brought me up out of the chute and held me upside down, my braids dangling to the floor. Way down the hall I saw someone's small bare feet skid across the tile from the front door to the kitchen and then disappear. The boy who was holding me began to sway from side to side. This ding-donging increased my screams. The boys just laughed.

Suddenly, I saw two short legs in spaceman pajamas come charging down the hall, each stride full of strong purpose. The legs squared off at the knees of the boy who held me and kicked him hard. He howled and dropped me. It was Margaret, her face a furious red. Without even looking back at the boys, she grabbed my arm and dragged me from the house. We raced down the hall followed by the sound of the boys' protests.

Once in the yard, we stopped. Rock and roll music blared behind us, but no boy moved outside the house or called to us. The sky around us was clear of clouds, the moon a crescent. Tree branches waved; the neighbors' houses were dark. No one shouted; nothing fell; no sirens. I shuffled my feet on the rough grass. The night breeze felt like quick fingers on my legs. The wind rose and moved the ends of my hair.

Margaret took my hand and we ran down the warm sidewalk, past the empty garage, on to the next block. We jogged in triumph. I saw the two of us in a newspaper photograph come to life: Wearing matching baseball caps, our faces brown from the sun, Margaret and I would trot down the street in time, waving to our cheering game-show audience. Now Margaret brought me to a redwood fence where I looked between the slats at the water in her pool, shining and shifting in the light from the street lamp.

Margaret opened the gate and rushed to the side of the pool. I walked up behind her. She didn't bother to take off her pajamas, but simply dropped into the shallow water.

She stood neck-deep and brave in the pool, squinting up at me and giggling. I couldn't see the bottom, but I imagined something down there holding Margaret up to me. If someone were to draw me at that moment I would appear as a flash of bright light, an arc of fire from the sun, lighting up the dark.

Margaret punched and pinched at my ankles. "Come on, Scaredy Cat, jump in," she said.

Dizzy from the witchcraft of my true name finally uttered, I laughed and threw myself forward, diving headlong into the dark water.

The
Whole
Numbers
of
Families

Iris and I live outside Boston in a tiny apartment that we originally rented for its large windows and good light. We can barely get to the windows now, though, because the floor in front of them is cluttered with stacks of books, papers, photographs, and elusive letters from my mother. Sometimes I kneel on all this mess and watch the people go by in the August heat, three stories below. I see a lot of women, and even a few men, walking hand in hand. I'm not alone in my love for Iris, that is apparent. But these other people have different freedoms. They don't have narrow, barren families, or histories of not being able to express, or even imagine, what they want.

Iris often argues with me on this. She says, "You know, Marie, we all struggle. Then we grow stronger. Didn't your mother teach you that?"

"It's that last part I have trouble with," I say. "The growing stronger. She never told me about that."

Lately I feel weaker because my mother's in the East now, pulling strings. In June, Iris and I took her to the Rhode Island shore, a place she used to visit with her sister Berkie, and where she and I vacationed with my father years ago, before he died. When we got there, I found myself sapped of strength, hanging around behind my mother like a sulky adolescent, waiting in vain for her to grant me permission to think for myself. My mother spent most of her time in a lawn chair on the beach smoking cigarettes, raising a cloud between her and the rest of the world, so she wouldn't have to see Iris and me as a couple, or remember Berkie's recent death.

The three of us visited my mother's Aunt Lena. We stood around the ancient woman's bed as she tried desperately to identify us. Her face puckered, her brow scarred in confusion, she finally gasped, widened her eyes, and called out, "Porter?" My mother—in a predictable and deliberate fantasy—heard her own name being called, and she decided to stay. Iris and I left my mother in Rhode Island at the end of that week, the phone receiver hugged to her head while she fired the home care nurses and Meals on Wheels, and wound herself up into a tornado of order and duty.

My mother's in the East now, and she sends to Chicago for her things. She opens up Aunt Lena's spare room and fills it with her thick paperbacks, house dresses, and sale cartons of cigarettes. I fuss on the telephone with my mother and in the apartment with Iris. Neither is happy with me.

I feel safe at work, though, at the private high school where I'm an admissions counselor. I interview applicants for the fall term and marvel at the way the girls hide behind their curtains of long hair, shy and indifferent. They walk the halls with their parents, but they stare out the windows and seem to count the steps from the classrooms to the outside doors—they're already growing away alone.

Iris and I go out to dinner and the movies, where I refrain

from talking about my mother. I sit in dark theaters with my arms around Iris, holding tight. We seem hopelessly alone ourselves, I sometimes think, like Aunt Lena and my mother, all of us skirting each other trying to find the easiest way in, or at least the safest route out. I think about this when I call my mother in the middle of August to check on Aunt Lena. Every question about my great aunt is a cover; I'm really trying to get some reassuring words from my mother, but what they might be I haven't a clue.

"What about that name she called out?" I ask. "What about Porter?"

"Who knows," my mother answers, blowing out cigarette smoke. "When are you coming to visit?"

"I have a job, Mother."

"We all do, Marie. Aunt Lena is your oldest living relative."

"She doesn't even know me. I just want to find out how she is."

"You can't find out many things from Boston," my mother says.

I hang up, depressed, and wonder about secret messages, my mother's favorite form of communication. I do know my mother is angry. She has approached my love for women as if it were a foreign body, something separate from the rest of me. She sees me flickering like Edison's new electric light, like a new idea or invention that's startling and unstable, with dangerous potential.

"She's trying to make you feel guilty," Iris says that night. "But why!" She looks around frantically, as if she is being threatened from several directions. "You've been a good daughter."

"Iris," I say.

"You've indulged her in this Aunt Lena thing, helped bury Berkie. What more does she want?"

"Iris, I'm gay."

"You've been a good daughter."

*

As the weeks go by, Iris and I find we have less to say to each other. We practically live at the movies, silently holding hands while all sorts of stories go by on the screen—violent, romantic, desperate—and we hope they'll spark some new thought or inspire conversation. Instead, we ride home in dead, uncomfortable silence, which drags at my stomach. I feel a gritty sadness, a hopelessness, while the streetlights flash by our moving car. There is something familiar about this sadness, though, something clean and final, like the resignation my mother must feel in dedicating her life to the care of an elderly woman. No one can fault you for it.

Iris and I have stopped making love. Iris is a hot form next to me every night, luminous, brown-eyed; I feel warmth from her small head covered with black curls. Yet I have become the space left when someone is gone. Every time Iris turns and flings her arm I'm amazed it doesn't strike right through me.

"When I was five," I begin one night, trying to reduce the tension. I turn to face Iris.

"How old are you now?" Iris murmurs, her eyes glittery slits in the dark.

"I'm trying to tell you a story," I say, exasperated. My childhood waits to be reeled out, examined.

Iris moves up so close to me I can feel her breath dampen my eyelids. She clutches my hand and waits, ready to move at the first sign that I've returned to my life with her. Tonight, probably out of desperation, she touches me. The fan roars. I feel Iris's cool hand on my hip and her strong fingers stretching over my skin. I suck in my breath—this is not what I expected after such a long dry spell. What I feel is my mother, all the power of her years, her blood in me, the censure behind her mild eyes. Iris moves her hand down my thigh. I concentrate so hard on what she's doing, where she's going with her hand and how her light touch barely dents my skin that I don't realize I'm crying until Iris stops and brings her hand to my cheek.

"Marie," Iris says. She sounds impatient, and the possibility of this makes me cry harder.

"What's stopping you?" I ask, though I know.

"What's stopping me, Marie? Jesus." Iris sighs. "Where are you? I can't see you anymore." She presses her palm against my forehead.

"I can't give myself over," I say. I feel the tears start again. "What am I afraid of?"

"It's your mother, Marie. That's obvious. And you've had doubts about us all along." Iris throws back the sheet and stomps off to the bathroom.

It's June again, and I am on the beach between my mother and the sea. I smell the salt, feel it sting my lips; my mother stamps out her millionth cigarette. The surf sucks back. Iris swims, thrashing farther into the ocean, her arms and legs easy in their fight with the waves. She's moving like my mother's heart, which furiously works itself away from me.

I clean. This is my clearest duty at Aunt Lena's, and one that I can fulfill blindly. My mother, the headmistress, hands me buckets and rags, brooms and mops. I clean the bathroom until there is no trace of Aunt Lena there; I leave everything sweet-smelling and shiny and put all of Aunt Lena's medicines in a bag next to her bed. My mother's room is off limits. She leaves the door closed like a tightly shut mouth.

When I left Iris just a few days before, she kissed me good-bye right out on the street. "Come back," she whispered in my ear, and I jumped. She had a thin smile and hooded eyes and she looked away from me as she walked to our apartment. Once in my mother's shadow, though, I think of Iris only sporadically.

Instead, each circle of my arm with a dustcloth or each push of the mop reminds me of my childhood. We had been to this same resort town when my father was still alive. Berkie had stayed with us that summer—this was before her house was built—and my mother spent nearly all of her time with her sister. This left my father and me alone on the beach, me with my sun hat and beach pail, he on the chaise longue, thin, pale, his eyes rimmed with dark. As I remember him now he was somehow inorganic. His half-nakedness, his pale skin—he's more of a statue of a father now, an unbreakable slab in my memory, perhaps because he died before I could know him as more human. I realized later, of course, that his silence behind me while I sat flinging sand at the gulls was an attempt at closeness; he knew he was dying away, but he wanted to leave at this almost imperceptible speed. My mother, though absent, seemed to be circling my father with worry. Her abandonment, I later imagined, was a claim on my father's love. Don't forget me, her absence said; you can't leave without giving me all you have.

Right now, my mother pushes furniture against the wall in the next room. It is this that I hear most clearly, but it is not a reminder of duty, really. I am here at Aunt Lena's as a kind of submission. I have given in, made a sacrifice to my family. I'm not supposed to love Iris anymore, though that isn't working; at the very least I am supposed to give up a great deal of happiness, no matter what the source.

"When you were at the store earlier," my mother begins, dragging her bucket and mop into the middle of the living-room floor, "that girl called."

"What girl? Iris?"

"Yes. I said you were away."

"Is she going to call back?"

"I told her you were busy."

"Mother, I'd like to talk to her. I live with her."

"You're here now." My mother is practically throwing her mop across the floor with each stroke.

"That was a terrible thing to do," I say.

"Go ahead, Marie. Pretend knowing this girl is the same as family; pretend it's as important. You are so foolish. I don't think you know a thing about what ties people together. You're just flailing around."

I feel like a child again, small, weightless, like a piece of dust my mother can wipe away. Tears well up in my eyes.

"Go ahead and call her," my mother says to the mopped floor. "I'm not cutting the phone lines. I don't see you running to call her."

My mother feels me come up behind her, and, without looking, she hands me her mop so that I can finish the job.

The next morning my first sight is Aunt Lena, slumped in a stiff chair across from the couch. She is somewhere in her wretched state between functioning and unconscious, wearing a rude stare. A shawl dangles from her skinny shoulders. I think about how well she fits into our three-woman family: She's incommunicative, deadened, full of denial.

My mother comes through the room. "It's late," she says. "I've already got most of Lena's bedroom out on the porch and we've got to get her onto that couch."

I slide from my makeshift bed, my eyes constant on the staring Aunt Lena, then peek out the front door. A mattress leans against the porch railings, and in the side yard the clothesline is crowded with sheets and pillowcases. It heaves in the wind like a giant ghost.

Later that day I help my mother ransack Aunt Lena's room. We're looking not for valuables but for items full of old memories that we can throw away. This is my mother's idea. We go through the closet first but find only old boots, shoes, and purses, and a game of Scrabble with half the pieces missing.

"How many times do I have to do this?" my mother asks, sniffling.

"What do you mean?" I throw a pair of clunky red pumps on the discard pile.

"These could be Berkie's things."

"Oh, Mama," I say, and put my arms around her.

"Enough," my mother says, and leaves the room.

I start on the old secretary desk that sits in the corner of the room. In it I find electric bills from 1958, entry cards for contests, laundry tickets, a Norwegian newspaper in which all the women in the photographs have beehive hairdos. There are fountain pens and paper clips and tiny pencils with chewed erasers. There are no lists of addresses or any will, deeds, leases—nothing to indicate Aunt Lena had connections to the outside world. I put all the stuff in a pile in the middle of the floor so my mother can go through it and decide if she wants anything.

I go to Aunt Lena's dresser and haul open all the drawers. They're swollen from the heat and humidity. I lift out huge, loose pairs of white nylon underpants, some pinned at the waistband. Next is a silk kimono, which seems far too frivolous for Aunt Lena. Under the kimono I find a stack of letters secured with a decaying rubber band.

The paper is as dry as old skin, yellowed and cracked at the folds. The handwriting is ornate: curlicues, massive capital letters with tails and scrolls finishing them off. I sit on the floor and shake the bundle over my lap; old photographs fall out and release a sharp, sour odor. This is what I've been waiting for. I gather everything together and speed out of the bedroom, past my mother in the kitchen, who's busy slamming clean glasses onto the drainboard, through the doorway into Aunt Lena's backyard.

The afternoon is like a hot bulb around me, glaring, almost suffocating. The massive andromeda and climbing roses close in on me from the sides of the yard. I crouch under a tree at the back of the lot and sift through the letters; paper whispers. The writing almost demands to disappear; each letter seems to be disintegrating in the sun as I hold it. For a minute I think I've come to bury or burn them.

I turn to the photos. They clutter my palms, thick and shiny. "Porter and me" I read on the back of each one: Lena and Porter sitting on a sandy beach wearing calf-length skirts and holding parasols, the legs of men in stiff suits behind them. In one photo Lena and Porter have their skirts raised and their stockings rolled down; they're laughing. Porter has her arm wrapped around Lena's shoulders. This is a long love.

Nothing removes like family.

It's October, the previous year. Iris and I are in a bar and she's teaching me to dance, like she's taught me to do everything else. She puts her hand on my hip and then my hand on her hip, we sway from side to side, she stares at me until I smile—and my smile is another step. I circle Iris's neck with my free arm and pull her head close to kiss her cheek. Iris pulls back, smiles, and shakes her head—I've gotten too close too fast. Now, at Iris's lead, we sway back and forth again, our hips crashing together. The music is full of steel drums and twangy guitars and an insistent, synthesized noise like spurts from a blast furnace. Our calves are wiry roots, clinging, our thighs pull up and rest against each other, hips crash again. Now my arm circles Iris again and it's right: We meet. There is no longer a clear sheet, like water, between Iris and me, something I feel even when we make love. Instead, my passion for Iris is a sash that circles us both, the feeling of love embodied. I vow to take it with me everywhere, like an insanely happy puppy on a long leash.

But nothing removes like family. On that dance floor, I am dragging this bad dog behind me because it's something I couldn't learn outside the considerable shade cast by my mother. There she is again behind my closed eyelids, not a breath of wind or spark of light around her, though she's roaring bright. She's planted firm, motionless, turning everything off. My mother has become a valve in my heart and she lets nothing out. I am left with this: Iris and I are in love, dancing, moving under the flashing lights. We are a picture of something deeper, a representation of some indecipherable, secret feeling.

Now I'm yelling at my mother, though she's only three feet away. We're in her bedroom. It's late, and I've been obsessing over love letters between Porter and Aunt Lena for hours. I'm full of news of childbirths, deaths, crop failures, long, sad remembrances, and the intense missing of women apart. My skin is sour with sweat, my mother's cigarette overloads the heavy night air.

"You've gone too far this time," she says. "For heaven's sake, Marie, Aunt Lena was married." She's building a pile of ancient corsets on her bed next to some old wigs and a tangle of thick, pink orthopedic hose. Her room is a surprising mess: dirty clothes everywhere, overflowing ashtrays, the drape hem coming down.

"I know she was married," I say. "It was an escape." From the dresser, my mother's framed photo of Berkie smiles out at us with endless cheerfulness.

"You can just give me the papers and I'll put them in a pile with other things from the desk." My mother holds out one hand while she sorts, not even looking up.

"This is not a 'discard,' Mother," I say, sitting down on the opposite side of the bed. "This is a 'save.'"

I imagine this house in its own individual darkness. The night is really a curtain, dotted with clicking and whirring bugs, covering the open windows. The rest of the world refuses to surrender and bustles under the constant glare of the sun. My father and I are behind the curtain, under this sun, walking back from the beach years ago, his hand covering mine while I skip and stir up sand on the road. My mother and Berkie walk ahead. My mother carries a bucket half-filled with shells. Berkie smiles and chats, always "up," her attention on her older sister. I'm studying my mother from behind. She swings her bucket as if no one is watching her, a movement that is inconsistent with her serious housecleaning clothes— Bermuda shorts and a turban with flapping ends; she has no real beach clothes. She and Berkie laugh, and when my mother stops to catch her breath I see her look up and to the side, full face to the sun. It was startling: my mother turned away from my father and me, turned out of our small family as if we weren't there; my mother enjoying a separate life with her sister. My mother, myself, Lena, Porter, Iris—all our number— I'll string us together like the beads of a necklace and make us complete. We'll add up to something to remember, something to save.

"Mother, you miss Berkie a lot, don't you?" I now ask quietly.

My mother stares at me for a few seconds. "Oh, Marie, that's sick," she says. "Don't be so crass. Or desperate. I don't know what you are."

"I'm lonely. Don't you ever get lonely?"

"I got over that long ago. Your father died so many years ago." My mother rearranges the pile she's working on. She knocks it over and starts again.

"That's not what I'm talking about, and you know it," I shout. I gather up Aunt Lena's letters and photographs and head for her room.

"Marie, drop it," my mother calls.

Aunt Lena's room is stifling; the air feels yellow and thick, wrapped tightly like the old woman's blanket. Even after all the cleaning there's still a lingering odor of urine and hand lotion. I sit on the bed, my hands full of evidence. Aunt Lena dozes, her skin smelling of buttery dough. I nudge her awake.

She rolls her befuddled eyes to the ceiling, then down to the photo I am holding—Lena and Porter giggling on the beach.

Aunt Lena's head glows on the pillow, her sparse white curls translucent, her face a nest of sharp wrinkles.

"Marie!" my mother shouts again from her room.

But I'm on my own now. I feel as if I'm waiting for a famished dog to eat, anticipating my own satisfaction at her longed-for chance to fill herself.

Aunt Lena stares at the picture hovering in front of her. She has searching eyes, colored and smoothed like huge pearls. But no response, no recognition.

"Porter, Aunt Lena," I whisper. "You remember Porter." The globe-like eyes see nothing; she's looking right through me. "You've been asking for her," I continue, "and here she is."

I gather the photos back into my lap, knock them on my knees, get the corners straight. The crime is in forgetting, I think. My love for Iris, a long rope leading to the ground, slides out of my reach.

But what has Aunt Lena got to tell me? She must feel as if she's been dreaming under her own bed. The air is filled with the angry sound of my mother's footsteps in the hall and a dim, slanted light. There's a fuss about something, but Aunt Lena's so tired. The safest place is here, the dark home where she can forget.

"Marie," my mother says softly from the doorway. She looks confused, sad, even lost. She's holding one of Aunt Lena's old lace handkerchiefs.

Aunt Lena's fingers worry the edge of the spotless sheet and she stares straight ahead. I shuffle the photos like flash cards in front of her face.

Incognito

The only way I was able to afford a one-bedroom apartment, especially in Chicago's Near North, was through the generosity of my grandmother, who left me fifteen thousand dollars when she died. The money came in May, while I was living at my parents' home in the suburbs, a bland ranch house I was forced back into by layoffs on the Keebler cookie packaging line.

My grandmother's money also satisfied me psychologically by giving me an opportunity to infuriate my parents. A few days after I moved back in, I had announced to my mother and father that I, their only daughter, was gay. A week later, the day my grandmother's check came in, they glared at me all the way to the bank and then to the car dealership where I bought my new Toyota. Then they sat in the backyard the whole day I moved out my belongings, holding drinks and staring hard at the flowering lilacs.

After a week in my new apartment, which was in a quiet and dirty neighborhood full of other gay people, I began to think of my unemployment and idleness as something rather ethereal—an image, actually. Unemployment was the stunted maple tree outside my bedroom window, green and glowing in the late morning summer sunshine. The tree was the first thing I saw when I woke up and it heralded a new and empty day stretching out before me. I would see the tree, feel the Chicago humidity rally around my body, and I would close my eyes to daydream about all the leisure activities I wasn't enjoying. Something that was very real, however, was my loneliness. It caused me to stare dry-eyed every day at all the men and women loving each other on TV.

Early one morning I woke to the sound of someone dragging boxes up the building stairs. When I looked at my talismanic maple, I found a white cat teetering on the upper branches. It opened its mouth to meow, but didn't make a sound. I got up, put on an old T-shirt and running shorts, and opened my apartment door.

A woman lurched down the hall, hauling one end of a futon mattress. She pulled and then paused, pulled and paused, as if she were heaving up a sail on a huge boat. Her ash-blond hair just swept her well-muscled, freckled shoulders. She was at least a head taller than I was and wore a jogging outfit and sneakers; her feet looked as big as paddles. I followed behind her as she entered the apartment next to mine.

"Is that your cat?" I asked from her doorway. She already had a print hung on the wall, a red silhouette on white of a woman throwing the shot put.

"What cat?" She threw down one end of her futon and kicked it.

"This white cat I saw looking in my window. I've never seen it before and I thought it escaped. My name is Abby, by the way."

"Theresa," she said, smiling, as she walked over to shake my hand.

I had rarely shaken hands with a woman before and the politeness and briskness of it shocked me. Theresa had a quick grin and small, sly, green eyes. She stood with her hands on her hips, breathing heavily. I leaned on the door frame.

"That's Binky," Theresa said. "I let her out so she could get acclimated."

"This is not a good place for cats," I said. Had I read this? There were cats everywhere as far as I could see. "The little boys down the street like to throw rocks at any animal they can find."

"Binky's tough," Theresa said. She smiled, dismissing me, and turned away.

A few days after Theresa moved in, I was on the front steps of the building, getting ready to leave for a job interview. Theresa flew down the stairs and raced to her car, then off to work. "Hi," I called after her, but she was already halfway down the street. I thought of Theresa all the way to a local bank, where I failed my secretarial skills test, and even on the way home. She was sure to be too busy, important, and pretty to be available. I imagined her at her office, teeth gritted, her mind racing through deals, women and men falling at her feet. She would not be interested in a woman who made thirty errors in a sixty-second typing test.

I had a college degree in anthropology, unused, so my strongest skill, I thought, was overlooked. What set me apart from the average job seeker was my ability to see the meaning behind common ritual. I could bore through difficulties with merciless analysis. I knew the petty meaning of my parents' social prejudices and had experienced firsthand the hollow moments between men and women. Now, in coming out, I would enter a matriarchy—return home to a symbolic womb. Sisterhood. Love. Emotional riches. I knew the danger, however, of discussing new discoveries while one was in the field—it tainted one's findings. I'd made that mistake with my parents. Now I would watch silently as the secrets of this world were revealed. I would wander among the natives. I would bathe in the gay waters of Chicago.

Oprah Winfrey had voyeurs on her show the morning of my bank interview, busily confessing their sins. All the guests had been placed behind screens and had electronically altered voices. One man admitted to Oprah that he had had a normal childhood, no hanky-panky, until one day—bang!—he found himself looking through his sister-in-law's bedroom window. Oprah conjectured that this came from the man's frustration at not feeling loved. A woman in the audience insisted that this frustration had an unacceptable manifestation. The man and Oprah agreed.

"It's your way of saying, 'Me! Me!' I would bet," the woman offered. "By just looking you don't have to worry about interaction and you can still get what you want."

"Yeah, yeah," the man agreed. "No-fault love."

I would have Theresa over for dinner. I decided to do it on Wednesday so I could give the illusion of being too booked on the weekend to have her over then. That night I washed my hair and let it dry into ringlets and I even put on clean clothes, then I ventured down the hall to Theresa's apartment. I felt like Andy Hardy.

She answered the door with chopsticks in her hand. I smelled soy sauce. "You're eating," I said.

"Yeah. Would you like some? I made a lot."

"No, thanks. How's Binky?"

"Okay. She brought in a baby squirrel yesterday."

"Oh, jeez. Hmmmm. Well, I came here to ask you to eat again, Wednesday, at my apartment. I can tell you about the neighborhood."

"I thought you just moved in."

"I did. Last month. But I'm very observant." I wondered if this was flirting.

She smiled. "Sure. I'd like to do that. Can I bring anything?"

"Binky can come if she wants. I'm starting to miss animals now that I live in the city. I'll see you. You can come at six." I turned abruptly and left.

For the next three days I cleaned my apartment, throwing out newspapers, sniffing and discarding at the refrigerator, and vacuuming while Theresa was at work. I liked to think that I was cleaning out some deadly toxic debris left over from my youth in the suburbs. But my actions remained exactly what they were: attempts to look good on the surface when I fully intended to remain cluttered underneath.

For one thing I didn't know what rules to follow. Theresa was entering my territory, so I could watch her and learn about her, but there was also the chance that she'd be interested and would look back. What would she see? Every day without fail my mirror offered up a very round-eyed woman with bushy, dark, curly hair and a skinny, shapeless body. Theresa would see someone watching her, waiting for the go-ahead to be in love, waiting for the confirmation that she'd made the right choice. It had to be too much responsibility for one person.

She stood in my doorway on Wednesday, looming beautiful and large, and clean too, in red shorts and a white T-shirt. Binky hung over one arm, her eager eyes roaming my apartment.

"Here you are," I said. Then I talked very fast. In fifteen minutes I told Theresa about the layout of the neighborhood; about Max, the gay man across the street whom I had met; the landlord, a Norwegian immigrant who had a potato patch behind the building; and the weather for the next week.

"Abby, good heavens," Theresa said, laughing. She sat down on my couch, setting forth a cloud of dust. Binky ran over to my potted palm and dug away in the dirt.

"I thought you were working nights," Theresa said. "I never

saw you. And I knew you didn't leave for work in the morning like I did."

"I don't have a job right now, though I'm looking. I've got some money saved up."

"Oh." Theresa nodded and rubbed her thighs with her palms.

Someone once told me that people with cash use it as a buffer against intimacy. I suddenly wished I were anyone else, and smiled. "What do you do, anyway? Binky looks so sad when you go off in the morning." The cat clawed her way across the bottom of an arm chair and hung there, staring at me from upside-down.

"I'm an assistant loan officer at Continental Bank. They keep telling me I can move up." Theresa smirked.

"Not bad. That's my bank, actually. I like the high ceiling." I sniffed the air. The dinner was burning, but I didn't want to move.

Theresa laughed again. "Need a loan?"

I thought for a minute of the possible benefits of knowing a lesbian loan officer. Loans for houses that two women could buy together; remodeling loans to prepare for the baby you both could adopt; money for trips you and your lover could take to Greece where you would stomp around ruins, getting sunburned while looking for goddess remnants.

"No offense, but something smells funny," Theresa said.

"Enchiladas," I said. I ran to the kitchen.

The dinner was crispy, but saved. Binky sat at the window all through the meal and silently mouthed up a storm at the sparrows. I got a stomachache as I took my last bites because I wondered what to do next. Show slides? Talk about family? Friends? Feminist theory? Discuss Lévi-Strauss? Margaret Mead? We could always look through my old books for color plates of ancient Amazon axes.

Theresa had crossed over to the couch and now sat next to me. She kissed me on the lips. "Hi," she said.

I always wanted to believe that I had one of those lives that could be changed in a split second, that I was someone who would be present at the dawning of a momentous age or a great event. Here was my chance, but I still didn't hear bells or see the coming of deities. I smiled at Theresa and waited.

She looked at me, puzzled. "Well?" she asked.

"Well!" I exclaimed.

Theresa nodded. "You haven't had many lovers, have you?"

"Women lovers?" I asked. I slapped my palm down on her thigh, hard. "Not many," I lied.

"How many?"

"Numbers matter?" I tried to look shocked; I knew numbers did matter. "None." I smiled.

Theresa kissed me again and Binky jumped onto my lap. I spread my fingers on Theresa's thigh but kept an eye open to watch for any change on her face.

Theresa didn't call me and I didn't call her over the next week, but I kept watching her comings and goings. She never glanced toward my window. What did it really mean now that I had consummated? Was the initiation over? Was I now a true lesbian? Or did I just have an isolated piece of excitement?

Everything—my intuition, the rare light and clear weather, even Binky and her escapades—kept telling me that I should get out and enjoy my new life. After all, I had been waiting for this for years. I had supposedly found myself. But a few days later when I sat, nervous and poised for another job interview, this time in a fancy restaurant, I remembered that the key to discovering one's new identity lay, of course, in intimate social intercourse with one's true subject. Instead, I was perched on a high-backed black velvet chair facing Frankie, a man with an enormous moustache and tiny eyes dashed with red.

"So, you're a college girl." Frankie sized me up. "Think you're too good to throw food around?" He tapped his stubby cigarette on the edge of an ashtray. When he laughed, his beautiful teeth parted for just a moment, then set themselves into a voracious display.

"I like to observe people, to learn from others whose lives are different from my own," I said, full of confidence. "The Masai of Africa, for instance, are brave warriors, very traditional and very fierce. Even given the enormous cultural differences separating them from us, we can still learn much about our own lives by studying theirs. One can see, even morally, what one lacks, where one could be stronger. A waitress must know these things. To watch customers, to be able to instinctively sense what they need; that's important."

Frankie nodded and looked thoughtful. "You ever waitressed before?"

"No."

Frankie fiddled with his cigarette pack, then got up and left.

I never told Theresa about these failures—I never told her anything. Instead, I watched and listened from my apartment, guessed her thoughts, studied her movements. Oh, how to proceed? Finally, Theresa must have gotten fed up with my silent vigilance because in late July she began to appear with increasing frequency at my apartment, sighing and rolling her eyes at me whenever I opened the door to let her in.

Out of guilt for never calling Theresa, I agreed to drive us to a women's bar, but I got lost three times along the way. I finally found myself inside a cavernous room, with a bar on one side and a dance floor in the back, surrounded by mirrors. Dozens of women gyrated to music with a heavy beat. I put on my sunglasses.

"Abby, for heaven's sake," Theresa said. "I'll go get us some beers."

I lolled next to a pinball machine.

"This is called coming out of the closet," Theresa yelled in my ear, handing me an Old Style.

"Where's my apartment? Where's my TV? Where's Binky?" I sipped my beer and looked around the bar.

Theresa waved. "There's Kathy!"

"You know people here?" I groaned.

A tall, blond woman worked her way over to us. She had a set of long, straight teeth, like one of the Osmonds. Kathy peered into my face. "Do you have an eye infection or something?" She tapped one of my lenses.

"I'm just incognito," I said. "I'm posing as an average person, watching from afar."

Kathy smiled and looked from me to Theresa and back to me again. We all smiled, like idiots.

"Would you like to dance?" Kathy finally asked. We danced to four songs. Toward the end of each one Kathy would go into a frenzy, moving faster and faster, until the song was over and she would stop and look around, wiping sweat from her face. Theresa finally cut in and I went back to the pinball machine.

A woman stood down at the paddle controls. When she saw me she moved closer and set down her beer. She had very short, red hair and one eyebrow that remained higher than the other, giving her a skeptical look. "You're Jenny's sister, aren't you?" she asked.

"No, I only wish. No sisters."

"You look like Jenny's sister. What's your name?" The woman knocked into me.

"Abby."

"I'm Bud Light."

"Who Light?" I leaned closer to the woman's face.

"Bud!" she yelled. "Bud Light. Get it?" She held up her beer and laughed.

"Oh, oh," I said, vigorously nodding. "You are what you drink."

"Yeah. I guess so."

Theresa and Kathy came off the dance floor, breathless and

laughing. I felt Bud's hand slide down my back and pinch my rear.

"Ow!" I cried, jumping away from the pinball machine.

Bud laughed.

"Jesus, Bud," Kathy said. "Have some decorum."

Theresa looked at both of us, me rubbing my butt and Bud smiling and sipping her beer. She took my hand and led me silently out of the bar. We left Kathy and Bud arguing at the pinball machine.

"You'll talk to anyone, won't you," Theresa said when we got to the car.

"I don't know," I replied. "Are you jealous or something?"

"You don't know who's good or bad, yet. You can't tell."

"I'm still deciding. I have to watch for signs." I sighed. "I hate going out. Something stupid like this always happens to me when people are around."

"People are always around, Abby." Theresa stared at me for a minute. "It doesn't matter." She leaned over and kissed me, then fell back in her seat. I started the car.

My mother called me in the middle of August. I had had fair warning of the call in the form of a postcard of Grant Wood's *American Gothic*. On the back she had written, "We love you very much. Are you happy in your new lifestyle? We will call, okay? Love, Mother and Dad."

"Lifestyle!" I said to my mother on the phone. "This is no lifestyle, this is my life."

"Whatever you say, dear. Your father and I would like to see where you live—if it's safe. Chicago is so dangerous, you know." My mother, miles out in the suburbs, hadn't been to the city for a good twenty-five years, not since the South Side riots and the appearance of a new arm of the Eisenhower Expressway.

"I'd rather come to your house," I said. "And I'd like to

bring a friend for dinner." Theresa was tactful and sociable and pretty, and an assistant loan officer. She was probably the best lesbian I could bring; besides, I was pretty sure I loved her.

"Male or female?"

"Mother."

"I was just asking. Hold on a minute."

I heard mumbling. My mother got back on.

"Your father wants to know is she the kind to drink beer. He says he can lay in a case if she is."

I didn't say anything.

"We'll look for you both at five on a week from Saturday, then," my mother said.

I was up late the next night, watching an old movie while Binky prowled my apartment. I was shocked that Theresa had left her alone all day, so I gave the poor animal the crusts from my pizza, which she pounced on and juggled for a while, then ate. Something rustled at the door but I couldn't see anything past the blue of the TV. A note lay on the floor. It was from Theresa, inviting me to a celebration party at her apartment on Saturday. I could bring friends. The note ended with, "Where's my cat?"

This would be my chance to tell Theresa about my parents. I could also look forward to a room full of strange women, maybe even some from the bar. What would I wear? What would I say? I could see myself drowning in an ocean of women, going down slowly, a terrified smile on my face.

I took my six-pack of Old Style down the hall at about ten on Saturday and walked into Theresa's small apartment, which was already packed with women. The only men—Max from across the street and another guy I didn't recognize—waved to me from across the crowded room. Theresa was nowhere in sight.

I wedged myself into a corner and opened a beer. A clump of women stood around the windows smoking joints, while a couple held each other and danced slowly, even though Janet Jackson blasted from the speakers. A few women looked at me and smiled. Theresa came around the corner from the kitchen and caught my eye, then held up a finger and went back into the kitchen.

Max and the other man made their way over to my corner. Finally, someone to talk to.

"I never see you," Max said, shaking his head and rattling my arm. "This is my lover, Steve. Steve, Abby from down the hall."

Steve smiled and shook my hand. He had warm eyes, like a counselor. He also had on a denim miniskirt and carried a clutch purse. New discoveries were in my face, with a vengeance. I tried not to stare.

"Have you known Theresa long?" Steve asked.

"Not long enough," I said boldly.

Steve and Max looked at each other and smiled. Steve scanned the party. "What a beautiful family I have," he said, sighing.

"I beg your pardon?" I asked.

"Steve sees us all as sons and daughters," Max explained.

"That way, I never feel lonely," Steve said. "And besides, I really think it's true."

"But you don't even know these people!" I cried. When I looked out at the party I didn't see people; all I saw were twenty or so complex, closed-off lives. Because intimacy made me so queasy I couldn't see why anyone would yearn for it in such large quantities. It was as if Steve were happily driving a car into a brick wall, over and over again, too dense to feel the pain.

"You have to look for what we have in common, not for what sets us apart," Steve said.

"Yeah, and besides," Max said, "look where most of our families have put us. Outside. They've closed the doors in our faces."

I stood there, dazed. As far as I was concerned, gay people

made up an amorphous, loose, happy group, pairing up for love but still remaining outlaws. This family business seemed too familiar and dangerous. An old idea like that made the present very confusing. Max and Steve each kissed me on a cheek and moved away.

I stood in my corner watching women kiss, hug, dance, drink, and smoke. They moved toward each other and then away, yet there was always something between them: a hand, a look, some sympathy, even if they weren't in a couple. Some women seemed to be sweethearts with everyone in the room. Theresa came out of the kitchen several times but she always got waylaid and ended up in a group of laughing women. Someone moved up beside me and I turned to see Bud Light, grinning up at me.

"Hi, there," she said.

I moved my back against the wall. "Do you want a beer, Bud?"

"Sure. Have you been here a while?"

"About an hour," I said.

"I'm getting bored. I know a lot of these people, but I had bad business with some of them. Do you know what I mean?"

I didn't have a clue. Bud seemed a lot less drunk than when I'd last seen her. "Do you know Theresa well?" I asked.

"Oh, sure. We were together a while in college, but we fought like dogs. We're antagonistic friends now, and that's fine with me. She's a good kid."

"I like her," I said, taking a deep breath.

"Ohhh," Bud said, nodding slowly. "Well." She grinned.

"Abby!" Theresa called. She was on her way over from the kitchen.

I waved and smiled. Bud guzzled her beer.

"I'm sorry I haven't been able to talk to you yet," Theresa said, grabbing my hand. "Are you okay?" She glowered at Bud.

"She's fine, for God's sake," Bud said.

"I've been waiting to talk to you," I said. "How the hell are you?" I squeezed Theresa's hand.

"Great. Work's going well, I'm healthy. Got good friends." Theresa gestured toward the party.

I felt very lightheaded and buoyed by the sight of Theresa. "My parents called me," I began.

"Who?" Theresa was surveying the party. "Oh, your parents. What have you been up to lately, anyway? I haven't seen you in ages."

"It was just two weeks ago you came over after work."

"I guess you're right."

"Well, my parents called, wanting to make up. They want to have me for dinner."

"That's wonderful!" Theresa was smiling only at me now. She seemed full of empathy. "They had to accept you sooner or later. Right? Didn't I tell you it would work out all right if you came out—joined the crowd?"

I looked around at the crowd I hadn't really joined. Everyone danced and talked and made friends, all involved in ancient rites that were mysterious to me. "So I'm going to my parents' house and I thought I'd bring someone," I said, still looking at the party. It was futile. This woman and I had made love, but we didn't know each other. She was nice enough to like me, but she had all this. And now, I realized, her empathy was just sisterly, or worse, motherly. Where could we possibly go from here? It was I who was the little-known friend invited to the family dinner, accepted only on the surface, out of charity.

Theresa looked worried and sad. She opened her mouth to say something to me, but I had already started to speak, almost shouting. "Look, I'm not asking you to marry me or anything," I cried. "It's just dinner. Just help me out a little. I've got to start somewhere."

All the women seemed to stop what they were doing to look at me. The party froze until I was the only active guest, embarrassed by my suffering.

Incognito

Theresa tried to hold my arm; Bud grasped my hand. But I drew back, getting ready to leave—maybe I could salvage some pride if I got out fast. Yet when I looked out at the room again, I saw a crowd of women's eyes, all of them familiar. They were telling me everything I didn't already know.

God
of
Gods

What had his family been thinking when they named him? Odin Tollefsen often wondered. What had they seen as they gazed into his crib? Odin swore he remembered each looming face: first, his father's red, sorrowful visage bracketed by muttonchop sideburns; then his mother's plump cheeks bunched into knots of pink, her mouth a perfect *O* of pleasure; finally, his three sisters' kite-shaped faces in graduated sizes, all hung with blond pigtails and matching scowls. Had they seen great promise? Secret strength? Perhaps because his immigrant parents had waited so long for a boy and here he was, the first child of the new Depression, the future man—and such a hefty baby!—they thought the grandest name was fitting, so they called him Odin after the supreme god of the Norse people, a magician of change, a conjurer of unlimited powers.

Odin became a man who carried a weapon of sorts, a cleaver, and he also learned his way around knives, hooks, meat saws, and hog scrapers. The pads of his fingers and the palms of his hands were crossed with crazy scars like lightning bolts. And in 1970, by the time he turned forty, Odin's seventeen years as lead butcher at the mammoth Jewel food store on North Avenue in Chicago had made him a man in charge of his own little world.

He had two Poles working under him, Kryzinski and Kowalski; Pavel, a Czech; Menker, a high-tone German; and Burke, an Irishman who claimed he was related to the Daleys. None of these clowns had ever heard the stories of the mythical Odin, of his wrath, his capacity for terror or beneficence, whichever he chose to exercise. They didn't even say his name. Nearly everyone at Jewel called Odin "Viking" because of his six and a half feet of bulk, his arms like hams, his pumpkin-sized head topped with thick, gold hair, his clear, blue eyes and rumbling voice; he was "Vike" for short. Only the black teenagers, who were strictly the baggers and shelf stockers, called him by his true name. "Hellooooo, Ooooodin," they sang out each day, as if calling to him from across a valley. "Ooooodin," they cried, as they curved around the ends of the aisles pushing their carts tipsy with boxes, their grand halos of hair shifting as they walked. Odin just blushed.

"Punks," Pavel said once.

"You wouldn't have caught them acting so disrespectful before all this power shit came about," Menker said.

Everybody had an opinion, even if it was stupid, and Odin noticed early on that the differences among the Jewel employees made for constant skirmishes. He tried not to care: As his dad had said, "Work, keep your mouth shut, and go on a good drunk once a month." To that Odin would add: Go ahead and run the world, just leave me the hell alone about private things. But alas, somebody was always coming around to tell you what to do with your days on earth.

"You need a woman to take care of you," Juliette from Bakery said in the middle of Odin's polite silence one day in that

summer of 1970, soon after he'd been named manager of
Meat. She was new. Odin had noticed that when he was alone
behind the counter Juliette silently appeared and began to
pace, pretending to look at chicken; he tried to will her back to
the cookie sheets and bread slicer.

"You need someone who can cook, a big man like you," Juliette continued, plunging her long fingernails into her crown of
teased hair, then fluffing. Did all women act this way? Odin
wondered. He tested Juliette's suggestions as he overlapped the
shrink-wrapped packages of fryers. He definitely wasn't interested. Not a bit. Cripes, he had his three sisters, and they were
enough women for ten men, always over at his house on week-
ends, rifling through his dresser and cupboards, peeking in his
refrigerator, hauling the Hoover from the closet. They
thought he couldn't manage either. Odin just grunted at Juliette. After that, she never came back to Meat, and Odin almost
forgot about her until a few weeks later when he found her and
Kowalski out on the loading dock in an embrace.

"And you a married man!" Odin said the next day, truly
shocked.

"Aw, you're just jealous," Kowalski said. "Aren't ya?"

Odin laughed and walked away. He tried to look restless
when the subject of women came up, restless or impatient, as if
he had no time for such trivialities. The alternative posture
would require his real feelings—fear and embarrassment at the
fact that women were not for him at all. He had a secret, one
that would bring trouble and blame upon him, though he'd
done little to deserve either. *I'm a man in love with men and
that's no calamity,* Odin thought in his better moments. And
what had he really done about it, after all? He'd dreamed of
one man, still unfound, and he'd wandered, looking, as anyone
would.

A few years back, on a walk one night in the park across Potomac Avenue from his house, Odin had found a water-stained
copy of *Mandate* flattened open against the base of a tree. He

took the magazine home, ripped out the ruined pages, and hid the rest of it behind the furnace in the basement, where he knew his sisters would never venture. He took the magazine out after work on Fridays in a ritual that involved ordering pizza, downing a couple of beers, and watching the comedy shows. He was like a regular guy at home, really, except for the magazine, full of the same photographs every week of biceps, stomachs, hard nipples, dicks, flashing past his face, jerky like an old movie. After a month, he knew these men intimately, knew every inch of them, and he felt he knew their personalities as well: This one with the curly hair and furry chest would smile and be kind to him; this one with the cleft in his chin would never say a word, but just walk away when the act was completed; this one with the thick thighs and faint crow's-feet would lie about his age, making himself younger just to please Odin; and this one, his backside to the camera, his spine and arms bent as if in pain, he would be faceless in person, someone to hate, someone to change the nature of sex. Odin rejected this image with a shudder. He'd had a few experiences in the army like that, quick and dirty, he and the guy pretending later that they didn't like each other, or had never met. And he had had a man like that once a few years ago in an alley not too far from Potomac, where he had been walking late one night, distracted, feeling floaty and removed from the quiet and the lights of houses. The man slipped up behind and brushed Odin's buttocks with his hands. Then when Odin turned, not too alarmed, it seemed, the man reached. He quickly muffled Odin's face in his corduroy coat. Odin smelled tobacco and booze as the man pushed him hard up against the side of a garage. Then the man's hands were on him, then warmth, red lights behind his eyes, then the man was gone.

In the fall of 1970, Odin's Jewel hired a new produce manager, a guy, unlike the others who were promoted, who came from a branch store. A stranger. Mr. Cushing, the store manager, brought him around and introduced him to each department.

"Mr. George Zapata comes to us from *Northlake*," Cushing said, as if workers from the suburbs were somehow better.

Everyone in Meat just stared until Odin finally stuck out his hand and said, "Tollefsen, Odin."

"Mr. Odin, pleased to meet you," the new man said, and smiled, shaking hands.

All the guys cracked up. "*Mr.* Odin, Jesus," Kryzinski whispered.

Odin watched George walk away. He was a medium-tall man, maybe five feet ten, with erect posture, thinning, shiny black hair, regular brown eyes, a medium build, maybe 160, but he had a smile like a window opening on the first good day of spring, that day when Odin's sisters came over and let in the fresh breezes and cleaned as if their lives depended on it. Odin felt his face redden.

"Oh, Christ," Pavel said under his breath, "now some Mexican."

"Yeah, what is this, the UN?" Kowalski asked, as they all walked back behind the counter.

"I think it's getting like one of those hippie SDS groups around here," Burke said. "Everybody welcome, *man*," he added, snapping his fingers and doing a little shimmy.

Odin was reeling the rest of the morning. You stood still for a second and then you could feel how fast the world was changing, and you could do nothing, like when he was a kid on his father's farm in Minnesota and he'd plop down in the pasture and watch the sky. Was it the clouds moving, or the earth underneath his body, or both traveling at once in some mysterious partnership? This George Zapata was a surprise, another shift. The new guy a Mexican, of all things, plus a man to turn another man's face hot, was just part of the whole crack-up of what Odin had learned to expect. Everyone's life was splitting open. Earlier that year, Burke's niece had met a black guy in college and started dating him; her father threw her out, so she had had to stay with Burke for a while until even he couldn't stand the sight of the two of them together. Then Pavel's kid was on the TV two years ago during the Democratic convention riots, a complete surprise to his parents, throwing a rock at a cop car and getting arrested right there, so he and Pavel hadn't spoken since; Pavel didn't even want the boy's name mentioned. And it wasn't just kids, either. Even Menker, who was pretty tight-lipped about his family, told them all on break one day that his wife had gotten hysterical the night before because of her housework and wanting a job and all, and when Menker refused to do the dishes she threw the good meat platter at him. He showed them all the bruise on his upper arm. "It's a damn sorry world when you can't tell up from down," Kryzinski had said as he looked over his half glasses at Menker's injury. But he, the oldest among them, had his own troubles: a son in college, the first in the family to go, who studied French, for crying out loud, no job in sight.

Several times that afternoon, Odin found excuses (which he made only to himself, halfheartedly) to visit Produce—an orange for lunch, a price check on potatoes for a Meat customer. One time, he began quickly stuffing a bag with apples because George had moved up next to him, clipboard in hand.

"Ah, a healthy fellow," George said. "I always say more fruits and vegetables and everybody would live to be ancient. Therefore my line of work. That one's bruised, brother."

"Oh, sure, ya," Odin said, putting the apple back on the pile. George grabbed it and slipped it into his apron pocket.

Odin felt impossibly nervous, jittery and sloshy in his stomach like something was about to spill out of him. His hands tingled. He drew a deep breath and glanced at George, who smiled with a lethal force. He had a flat, black mole in the middle of his left cheek. "So you live in Northlake, do you?" Odin asked, attempting heartiness.

"No, no. I worked in Northlake," George said, "but my family and I live on the Northwest side."

"Family?" Odin could hear the shock and disappointment in his voice. He had assumed—he wanted George to be alone, like he was—and something had told Odin that he was right, that George needed that string of talk and laughter between men as much as he did sometimes. He thought he saw George move a step closer, but perhaps that was just wishing.

"Yes, my parents," George said, "they're old—and my sister and her husband, we all live together. And you?"

Odin beamed. "I live on Potomac, across from La Follette Park," he said. "Alone. I have sisters, too, though. Three of them." He laughed and rolled his eyes.

"But what would we do without them, eh?" George shrugged and laughed, too. "You have a fine afternoon, Mr. Odin," he added, turning away with his clipboard.

"Oh, sure, sure," Odin replied, hurrying away with his bag of apples as if he'd just remembered an urgent task. The fruit grew heavier in his hands as he fled.

What were the responsibilities of a god, Odin wondered. What did the world expect of *him*? He watched his sisters on a September Saturday as they made their way through the drizzle to his front stoop, carrying Weiboldt's shopping bags full of freezer food. In the books Odin had read as a child, the gods created, destroyed, judged, and interfered in the lives of mortals, creating havoc by twisting fate. The gods also rescued mortals from what they saw as the mortals' foolishness, their endless limitations, because the gods were better, omnipotent, able to see backwards and forwards. Odin's sisters' husbands had parked the huge Oldsmobile in front of the house. Now the men lounged outside the car, lighting smokes and surveying the neighborhood, anticipating disappointment. There was no human like a god that Odin knew, no god-ness in anyone really, certainly not in him, just a fumbling suspicion about happy endings. Mortals were doomed, maybe despite the god-like ideas; you always fell short. Everything, everybody came up wanting because you had the all-accepting gods to remind you of perfection.

"This area's going down the drain," Odin's sister Sonja said, stepping into the front door vestibule.

"She's just noticing," Lillian said, following. She kissed Odin's cheek.

"Think of property value, Odie, really," said the third sister, Alma. "Resale and such."

"Oh, come on, now," Odin said, closing the door. But he stayed, looking out the little window, worried about his brothers-in-law. They were big, silent men, jokers when they did talk, lifetime steel mill employees who complained more and more lately about all the regular guys who were losing jobs to anyone who wasn't white. Propped against the side of the Olds, the three of them watched a black couple go by across the street. The man had an enormous Afro and wore blue jeans and an infantry jacket. The woman's hair hung in tiny braids down to her shoulders. She held the man's hand until they crossed the gaze of the brothers-in-law and then the man put his arm tightly around her shoulders.

Harlow, Sonja's husband, said something to Alma's husband, Craig. Lillian's Chester watched until the couple reached the corner and then he quickly turned, scanning Odin's street as if someone had called out to him.

Odin flung open the door and yelled, "The game's going to start! Hurry up!"

Chester and Craig spread out on Odin's couch, feet on the coffee table; Harlow, the oldest, took one La-Z-Boy, Odin the other. The Cubs were in Los Angeles.

"Beers!" Chester called to the kitchen.

"Please!" Harlow added, just in case.

But Lillian was already halfway to the living room with four cans of Stroh's in the crook of one arm, her other arm holding two stacked bowls of potato chips.

"Thanks, Lil," Odin said, cracking open his beer.

"Oooooo, don't you just love this man," she said, descending on Odin's face with kisses. "The women must eat him up! So handsome."

"Remember, Lillian," Chester said, "that's case closed."

"I know, I know," Lillian sang on her way back to the kitchen.

"Yeah," Craig said, "the man's too smart to ever get married."

"Wouldn't call him handsome, either," Harlow muttered, then belched.

Odin blushed. Just that morning he'd stood in front of the bathroom mirror, wetting his comb and wondering if anyone could consider him good looking. He had parted his hair first on the left, then on the right where it had always been, evaluating which way looked best. He had straightened the collar of his sport shirt. Big, big: everything about his appearance was oversized and pushy, in contrast to his personality. He didn't have a handsome face, comparing himself to the standards of old movie stars, like Fairbanks or Gable; no, his nose and ears, even his eyes, looked rough, half-finished, like hand-shaped features on a monument; against his will he loomed over people, daring them to notice him. That was no way to make an impression. He wanted to creep into people's awareness like a pleasant realization. Quiet. Welcome. Somewhere in Odin's mind that morning was a home full of soft sounds like blankets pulled across a bed, of kindness, a place that he entered stooping slightly, then rising to his full height to meet George Zapata, for Christ's sake. George's home was crowded with tiny, peppery people speaking rapid-fire Spanish. Odin carried a nice rib roast wrapped in white paper. Oh, they probably didn't even eat roast, Odin had thought, taking one last rueful look in the mirror and then switching off the bathroom light.

Odin and the brothers-in-law marked the seventh-inning

stretch by opening fresh beers and making trips to the bathroom.

Craig settled back on the couch a few minutes later and pointed to the TV. "Lookit, Ernie Banks has his own commercial."

Banks made a pitch for a remodeling company. He looked modest in his blue suit, quiet, thoughtful—Odin had always assumed he was a decent fellow. But when he smiled—oh!—you'd believe anything he said. Some people were like that, all emotion in the teeth and lips. Like George Zapata, giving you a way in, unafraid, every time he smiled. That approach was brave these days, with everyone so suspicious. Eyes never met on the street anymore because that could lead to words, or even fighting, no matter what your color. On TV, Ernie Banks's arms gestured like hands on a clock.

"Did you hear he ran for alderman?" Alma asked. She and Lillian and Sonja had arrived to pick up empties and to check on the game.

"Yeah, and lost," Chester said.

"Couldn't even win in a colored ward," Harlow added. "His own neighborhood."

"Well, he ain't no brain surgeon," Sonja said, and laughed. "Dumb as a brick, probably."

"Helluva first baseman, though," Chester said.

Banks faded out and now the Dodgers took the field. The cheery voice of Jack Brickhouse listed the previous innings' grim statistics. Odin chewed his lip. He couldn't let it go again. He had to say something; if he didn't, he felt part of himself erase with each one of their asinine comments, as if they were talking about him instead of blacks, Jews, whoever—as if they were somehow denying him.

"Sonja," Odin said, "would you say, 'Dumb as a brick' if Banks was white?"

The room exploded. "Awwww," everyone said, rolling their eyes.

"What if it was Santo on instead?" Odin asked. "Would you say it then?"

"Here he goes again," Harlow said. "Sonja, talk to this brother of yours."

Sonja shrugged. "Odie's always been tenderhearted," she said. "You never could say a word against anybody," Alma added, shaking her head.

Odin felt himself scaling that wall again. Every time he challenged their ideas, he'd get a foothold, move closer to the top, then face their indignation and slide back down again. And their bewilderment and patronizing! They thought he was dimwitted for the simple reason that he refused to share their views. They figured he hadn't yet learned about his own natural superiority to blacks and all the rest.

"You can't love the whole world, buddy," Craig said, turning his attention back to the game.

"But I don't have to look down on some folks just for no reason," Odin said. "Uff, you're all as bad as the fools I work with."

"No reason! No reason?" Chester shouted, sitting forward on the couch.

Harlow held his left fist up to his head, thumb and pinkie outstretched. "Hello, hello," he said into his little finger. "South Side? Get me Jesse Jackson. Yeah, yeah, that Operation Gimme Bread, Brother. Tell him Odin's calling and wants to join up."

"Ask if Jane Fonda's there," Craig said, his eyes still on the television.

"You listen to me, Odin." Chester poked his finger through the air over the coffee table. "Lillian! How long have we had the same mailman? Never mind, you'll take too long to remember. Anyway, it's fifteen years at least, and he's always on time, smiles, doesn't he, Lillian? That's right, never a problem. Two months ago, bang, a new mailman, colored. Old guy, too, walks slow. You know the type. So now we've gotten the neighbor's mail twice—twice!—he comes an hour later, Lil says, and, I've seen him, too—never a smile. Mean as anything."

"Won't say a word to me," Lillian said. "What have I ever done to him? And I said hello, too, just like he was anyone."

"And I'm thinking," Chester continued, "what if I get a check in the mail? Will it still be in the envelope later on?" He shook his head. "I don't know, I don't know. You've read the paper, seen the TV."

"What paper is that?" Odin asked. "What TV?"

Lillian said: "Our neighbor told us just the other day about these blacks that lure you into their bad neighborhoods and then rob you in your car."

"And how do they do that?" Odin asked.

"They stand in the street and tell you there's a detour and wave you down a dark alley to the thieves."

"I've read nothing like this in the paper," Odin said, laughing.

"Well then you're just blind, Odie," Chester said. "Really. Blind or—I don't know. Just open your eyes once and you'll really see," he added soothingly, as if to a child.

Anger was an uncomfortable feeling for Odin; it made him sour and clumsy. "Ambushes in the street!" he said, rising stiffly from his chair. "For God's sake. There's no talking to any of you." He waved away their complicated faces: fear, he saw there, and pity. "I'm going out for a cigar," he said. He hit his shin on the dining room table and continued on through the kitchen to the back porch.

The rain had stopped but now the air blew cold. Typical yo-yo Chicago weather. Odin lit a cigar. Two years back, when King was killed, blacks rioted and neighborhoods burned. Odin saw the whole business on TV: the breathless local reporters, the network veterans cringing as each cop car screamed by. All he saw of blacks on the screen were silhouettes, men and women throwing debris, smashing windows, yelling and crying before conflagrations. It was the sorest grief imaginable, Odin thought at the time, terrifying because of its surprise, the shock of a sudden eruption no one had cared to see building. Sitting now on the stoop, looking over his small, neat square of yard, Odin squinted, concentrated. Perhaps he could be omniscient, see the future come out of the past for blacks, maybe even for men like him. The sky was the seat of power, the source of change. Perhaps the weather, whatever direction it might take, could wear down his sisters and their husbands. They were just dry shapes, after all, just a mess of a structure about to tumble down. They were kindling for the fires to come.

On the last Saturday in October, a group of white kids met in Marquette Park, made a lot of noise about blacks and Mexicans and so forth, and then ran through the neighboring streets waving baseball bats. A half mile from the park they spotted a black man taking out his trash and one of the kids (that's what they were, really, kids too young for the war and too poor for college) whapped the black man on the temple with his bat as the crowd swooped by, and he died on the spot out in the alley next to his cans. They never caught the kid.

Odin worried about the incident all day Monday even though no one brought it up. On top of that, George Zapata had barely waved to him that morning, and that further depressed him. By the time Odin reached home that night he was exhausted and discouraged about all of humanity the way he got when he read the whole *Tribune* at one sitting.

After dinner, he stood on his slab of front porch and looked across at the park, empty in the cold twilight. Soon old Mr. Montoya from next door came out on his stoop and stood in his T-shirt and Cubs hat and droopy gray slacks, his hands in his pockets, and also surveyed the park in silence. He and his wife had only lived there a year; they were senior citizens who had fled a bad neighborhood for their first house. This information Mrs. Montoya had told Odin over the back fence last summer until her husband came and clutched her elbow, guiding her away without a word. Since then it had been just brisk nods and waves when the neighbors saw each other.

Odin cleared his throat. "It's a shame, isn't it," he said.

"What?" Montoya asked, startled.

"The colored fellow those boys hit." Montoya looked at him blankly. "You know, those white boys," Odin continued. "They killed a man. Marquette Park."

"Oh! Oh, yes," Montoya said. "That was a sad thing, very violent. My wife is afraid to go out of the house when she hears these things."

"You darn right," Odin said, eager to agree. "Especially for you folks."

"Ah, beg your pardon?" Montoya turned toward him now. His T-shirt stretched tight across the hard bowl of his stomach.

"Well, I," Odin began, faltering, then he shoved ahead. "Being Mexican and all, I would think you'd worry about the likes of them."

Montoya remained silent for a moment, hidden in a shadow. His eyes looked like dark, gouged-out surfaces, like weathered rock. Odin thought he saw Montoya's lips move. What language did the man think in? Was he translating Odin's words?

"We all should worry," Montoya finally said. "All of us who want to live peaceful." Then he abruptly turned back to the park.

Odin cast about for some statement that would make amends, though he had no idea what he'd done. "Now here's the thing," he blurted. "We have this new fellow at work, George Zapata? Anyway, he's the nicest fellow, hard working and all. And you wouldn't believe what some of the others say, just because this Zapata is a Mexican. As if that mattered." Odin paused. "For me, I don't understand that thinking," he added.

Montoya gazed silently at the park, lifted his face as if to look at the stars, then fastened his gaze on the streetlight. He scratched his shoulder, adjusted his Cubs cap. "Right now," he said, "in Cuba, where I'm from, it would be warm, flowers blooming, not this cold wind. My father had his own plants in the back: banana, breadfruit—just a little garden for his fun. You could hear the leaves rustle in the breezes and that would put you right to sleep." He stopped, took a deep breath. "Good night, Mr. Tollefsen." The aluminum storm door slammed behind him.

Odin worked on his cigar, trying to locate his mistake. I couldn't have been more straight out about it, he thought, breathless from the effort. You had to be so careful, even with the truth and good intentions! He felt a weak flicker of anger toward Montoya, but it never ignited. What did his neighbor care about his views as long as he kept his lawn mowed? For a moment he felt despondent, all his outgoing energy, his carefully laid path, gone to waste and neglect. Leave the future up to God, his mother always said. But how could God, any god, ever count on his will being done, seeing as humans were so unpredictable and wrongheaded? Surely no god had counted on these Marquette Park boys, pimpled and sweaty, waving their bats. No, people misread all the signs. You could put them on the trail to true happiness and peace, and still they'd turn and run opposite. No amount of calling could bring them back. So then you had the roads leading to goodness filled with the gods alone, at wits' end without the mortals and in despair, missing the humanity they had worked so hard to straighten out. You were better off mortal, it seemed, flawed like everyone else. It cut down on the disappointment, anyway. Odin pictured his mythical namesake, wearing Odin's own face and a coat of skins, shuffling along in his reindeer mucklucks, the lightning bolt and hammer he dragged sending up a quiet cloud of dust.

Odin flexed his scarred fingers. When he was a teenager the

air around him seemed to snap with possibilities like the bigger and bigger sticks he broke barehanded to test his growing strength. Today he was as big as he was going to get on the outside, and his eyes could see what those clowns at work or the boys on their rampage couldn't: that he was a man with the power of a tremendous secret, a man with hidden knowledge, a man prepared to smash his own life right open.

It wasn't the way he had pictured it at all. When Odin finally arrived at Lancelot's Books off of Rush Street (after driving aimlessly for an hour, chewing furiously on his lip, wincing at each swallow of Scotch from the pint under his seat, scanning the sidewalk for anyone who might recognize him—but who would know him *here*?), he found a drab, well, bookstore, a room the size of a corner grocery full of racks of faded magazines and paperbacks with lurid covers. Two other men browsed the material, and one man sat behind the cash register reading a fat book and smoking cigarettes. Somewhere a transistor radio bleated an old show tune. A squeaky swell of strings, a trip on the edge of the doormat, and Odin found himself smack in the middle of it all, the center aisle of the store.

It had taken him years to get here. He'd seen the address for Lancelot's in a magazine, even located the store on a map, but he hadn't dared to enter until now, until George had cast his spell. The *idea* of the man was so entrancing that it drove Odin to this kind of recklessness. He looked around the grim store, now an oracle's den. He wanted experience to bring back to George, something practical to marry to his sizzling desire, the materials needed for constructing their joint fates. The other two browsers in Lancelot's, much younger men, peered over the top of the front book rack at Odin, then shot their eyes toward the floor.

Even here you'd find embarrassed fellows. Who knew who

anyone else might be? Were they serious or pretenders? Threats? The reality of who he really was became so frightening to Odin at times that he went days without looking in the mirror, as if his homosexuality gave him devilish, silver-colored eyes or a face covered with warts and hair, or created some kind of troll or monster soul inside himself that he had to defeat. Lately, though, he saw something different when he thought of an enemy to conquer—something outside of himself, something shapeless and unclear, still unformed, something he knew these men, and others, saw too. A different quality of air filled Chicago now, expectant and strung tight, difficult to breathe. Everyone sensed it. Some nights Odin could feel this air squeeze him, even as he sat inside at the TV. It permeated his neighborhood, tossing the tops of the undressed trees, bringing people out to their front stoops at night in the growing cold to gaze at the moon as if it were a blank page on which a message would appear. Supposedly, the message was carried on the news, in the fights and riots, but it really resided in more personal pockets of anxiety and rancor. It seemed nobody knew where to look, what to do. You were always meeting someone halfway and then wondering if the space between you both was cool water to cross or the fires the other person wanted to burn you in.

Positioning himself before a rack in the bookstore, Odin reached for a magazine that had a black man on the cover wearing a telephone lineman's belt and a pair of jockey shorts. A bevy of shirtless men paraded through the magazine bearing the props of various jobs: power tools, spools of wire, steel-toed boots, sledgehammers, hardhats; one man even held an oscilloscope in one hand and a portable television in the other. Odin picked the magazine because of the photo of a redhead in crotch-ripped bell bottoms pushing a cart laden with bunches of ripe, bursting bananas. George Zapata, Odin thought when he saw the photograph, imagining his coworker's figure in place, his smile like a flash bulb lighting up the dark of Odin's imagination, George's hands gentle on the cart, the wheels shushing across the linoleum floor right toward Odin.

Odin moved down the rack of magazines, the one he'd chosen rolled up under his arm. He flipped through a few more, but they all looked the same: men, men, and more men, posed, flexed, and shiny, gazing into the long distance as if they'd lost something. No one looked into the camera. These men were like those isolated tribesmen who thought the camera was a god, a soul stealer. But you couldn't meet any man's eyes when you were a man like this, Odin thought, because that other body caught you, froze you, made you permanent and exposed with his look.

Odin felt someone move up beside him. It was one of the two younger shoppers. Odin had come to the end of the rack, next to a peeling green wall. The man's plaid coat sleeve brushed Odin's arm, pushing Odin further to the side. The man picked up a magazine and started flipping through. Then he stopped. Odin stood still, barely breathing. He could hear the man chewing gum, hear the guy's stomach rumbling.

The man stretched his arms to the side until the magazine was under Odin's nose. Odin looked down at the photograph of a young man, very broad in the shoulders like a swimmer, with a wide chest and a firm, blocked abdomen, standing before a white backdrop. He was blond and naked, his head turned from the camera and from the arm that reached from outside the frame of the photo toward the man's erect penis, held firmly in the model's own hand. A man's fingers could fit in the gully of thigh muscle on that boy, Odin thought. Some man's hand could test the firmness of his smooth biceps. Odin shifted his feet.

"See?" the man whispered.

He pushed against Odin until Odin's body pressed against the wall. Then he put the magazine back in the rack and slid one hand across Odin's stomach, fiddling in the buttons of his wool shirt. There were stacked, dented cartons, thick with dust, a few empty Nehi bottles, and a wadded-up rag between the end of the rack and the wall.

Odin felt himself worked upon; first the man's hands were in his shirt, next they were reaching up to caress his face. The lights in the store seemed as bright as those in an operating room. Who would want to see or be seen in here? Odin rested his cheek against the wall. It was George he wanted, here but not here, George who Odin wanted as physically present as he was emotionally. Instead here was another faceless man, in a hurry, furtive. And that furtiveness kept men like them hiding. The man's hand now moved down over Odin's crotch, fingers pressing. Odin couldn't bring this back to George. It was untested desire. Wasted. Odin felt himself emptying out, his mind dumping all it felt and knew with a whoosh, as the man grabbed at his pants.

The man moaned, drew closer. "Big fellow," he whispered to Odin. "Just like in the picture."

Odin's breath came faster, his mouth dropped open, then he found himself slapping weakly at the man's hands. He seemed to have no strength. "Nope," he said, his eyes closed. "Uh-uh." His hip rubbed the wall. "Naw!" he cried and pulled the man's hands away, then held them. They were thin and strong, with knobby knuckles. "No more!" Odin whispered, looking at the man for the first time. He saw a flat face, hooded eyes, any fool, any man, no distinctive features: butcher, baker, candlestick maker. The man's face closed down as quickly as he could turn back to the rack and open a magazine. He rolled his shoulders away from Odin.

Odin pushed past the man and stumbled down the aisle and up to the door, his head pounding, blood rushing, radio music tweeting in his ears, his heart filled with the terror of such an unfinished life.

On the same day in November, Pavel brought a gun to the

break room at Jewel and George Zapata saved Odin's life. The two incidents forced Odin to see that events in his life had become both delicate and dangerous, part of a battlefield strategy, like in Korea during the war. The army efficiency of cause and effect had impressed Odin more than anything: A call on the radio produced gunfire, or ceased it, then a march followed, then new talks among the leaders and rumors of peace. Fate could be brokered, controlled. But now Chicago seemed caught in a daily war with no discernible enemies or allies, just random malaise and disaster that attached themselves to people Odin knew and trusted.

The weekend before Thanksgiving, the white boys had massed again in Marquette Park, louder this time, joined by a few adults, too, and then some blacks countered by marching all the way from the South Side to Mayor Daley's office. Odin reasoned later that this weekend agitation had so rattled Pavel that he bought a pistol and hid it in the gym bag he brought to work. He first showed the gun around the break room on Monday, carrying the bag open by its handles in front of him.

"I'm ready now," he said to each person.

"Oh, Pavel, for Christ's sake," Kowalski said. He waved him away.

Burke was out front. Kryzinski and Menker just glanced in the bag and then continued sipping their coffee and scooping crumbs from a bag of pulverized potato chips.

Odin gasped, though the weapon appeared ineffective, even at rest. It looked like some old, greasy movie prop nestled in the spotless cotton of Pavel's after-work shirt. Something familiar, yet displaced, like that man's hand in the magazine photograph at Lancelot's Bookstore.

"What the hell is the matter with you?" Odin shouted, standing up. "Get that out of here!"

"Man's got to protect himself, Vike," Pavel said, zipping up the bag. "There's a lot happening out there and none of it's good."

"This is work. This is a grocery store. You've gone nuts."

"With all this bullshit, all these marches, you think I'm going to take any chances?"

"Is your skin black?" Odin asked. "Is it?" Pavel's gaze ticked around the corners of the break room. Had this man really gotten so loose, and without Odin's noticing? Pavel laughed, a little hiccup, and Odin's stomach lurched. He imagined a crowd of black people outside Mayor Daley's office, rippling like a dark cloth, and Pavel firing into the fabric, tearing it.

"Who's talking about blacks?" Pavel asked. "I don't care about them and all that uppity-uppity crap. It's whites I'm worried about. And I've got other problems, too. I'm a minority, you know. I'm Slavic. Who's to say we're not next? After all, the Nazis hated us."

"Pavel, your family's been here for a hundred years, so shut up," Menker said, turning a page of the newspaper.

"Listen to me now," Odin said. "I don't want you to bring a gun to work again. Do you understand?"

"Who are *you*?" Pavel asked, his face reddening.

"The manager of the damn department," Kowalski said. "Stop throwing your weight around. Now everybody be quiet. I'm trying to read 'Dear Abby'."

Kryzinski said: "I'm writing to 'Dear Abby' about this meat department. She'll never believe it."

Odin didn't speak to anyone for the rest of the day. Later in the afternoon he took over one of Pavel's tasks, cutting a forequarter of beef. He didn't want the man handling any semblance of a weapon. And Odin could do this in his sleep. First he used his knife along the twelfth rib to separate the plate from the rib, then to cut across the shank. To remove the plate and brisket he would have used the meat saw, but the tool was across the room, and there was something satisfying in holding the cleaver, so sharp, like a firm decision, a tool with a history. While Odin slammed down with the cleaver to make the breaks in the stubborn bone, he tried to manage the picture of

Pavel and the gun that was taking large shape in his mind. Odin had always assumed himself to be more or less like his fellow men, despite the nature of his intimate thoughts. So when he hired Pavel, and all the other meat cutters at Jewel, he saw no one much different from himself: regular guys, not too heavy on the genius, trying to make an honest living. But Pavel, the gun. You could do only two things with a gun: one, have it lie around so you could look at it as if it were a piece of art or furniture; or, two, fire it. And the fact that you got a gun in the first place meant that number two was a distinct possibility.

Odin hacked away. The bone wouldn't give and the meat cleaver felt floppy in his fist. Who was Pavel going to fire at? Who did these crazies, like Pavel and the kids in the park, who the hell did they think was after them? Cripes, men like that, Odin thought. He imagined Pavel shoving open the door of Lancelot's and opening fire.

George Zapata entered the cleanup room on the other side of the glass partition and smiled and waved at Odin. He walked up close to the glass.

"I got into some rotten stuff at the bottom of a case of green peppers," he yelled.

Odin nodded. George's voice was muffled, as if he were trying to speak with a hand over his mouth.

George pointed to his slick arms. "I have to use here to clean up because there's a mess over at my sink."

"Ya, sure," Odin yelled. He was conscious of his bloody apron and flushed face, too much red, too bright, way beyond what someone needed to be scared away. But George lingered, smiling. An open face. Nothing could shut it down, except maybe a declaration of love from Odin. Odin's stomach jumped, then his hand with the cleaver shook.

"Thanks," George finally said, then turned to the sink.

Odin stopped work to watch George. Maybe it was a job spent on fruits and vegetables, delicate things, that made George so precise. He turned on the water in the big steel sink and let it splash while he rolled up his sleeves another few notches. Odin watched George's arms emerge, tan, covered with fine black hair all going in one direction, muscles protruding like narrow elastic bands under George's skin, so unlike the stiff, bulging knots in Odin's own limbs. Odin let out breath, slowly, as George plunged his arms into the steaming water. Odin felt it, too. George worked on each arm vigorously, wetting and rubbing, then squeezing from the bottle of dish soap on the counter and working up a white froth.

What's he got on there? Odin wondered. He could take off his own skin. George stood with one khakied leg cocked, his narrow hips pressed against the sink. His shirt was white, pristine, like the shirt in Pavel's bag only George's shirt was for during work, not after; butchers couldn't keep anything clean. Sometimes Odin thought the inside of his house smelled permanently of iron, blood, and grease—a smell all too reminiscent of extreme appetites. George's labor had loosened a lock of his black hair and it lay curled on his forehead, bobbing as he washed. Now he reached for the deep-cleaning grease and smeared it up and down both arms.

Odin felt a stirring at the bottom of his stomach, and below, in his groin. The feeling invaded his blood and set it thrumming, as if a separate heart beat in each of his veins. He felt his face flush. He gripped the edge of the cutting table.

Oh, no, he thought. Goddammit. This was where he had left off in Lancelot's. Not here, not here. He tried to picture the unappealing man in the bookstore, but he saw only George's sinewy hands sliding up his arms, then down. Don't be stupid, Odin thought, trying to insult himself out of desire. Don't be a fool. This is work! The face of Pavel popped up again, and that gun on the white shirt in the white gym bag that dangled under his nose. Maybe everybody had a gun like Pavel did, at home, hidden; Pavel was just open about it. Maybe what they had at home weren't guns but ideas, thoughts, surprises, each like a black gun on white cotton. Just like Odin's own secret, dark against the light when it's exposed, and just as killing as a gun.

Odin picked up his cleaver again and brought it down with a crack on the bone. He saw an ivory shape shoot upward toward his right eye, like a huge snowflake on the wind. At the same time Odin tried to squeeze his eye shut to prevent the shape from entering. This is going to hurt like a son of a bitch, he thought right before he felt a scratch across the pinched corner of his eye like the swing of a needle over an old record, and then there was a boiling pain, colored red.

"Holy Christ!" he yelled, cupping his eye with both hands. He doubled over and started to dig at his eye, but that only reddened the pain.

"Dammit to hell!" he cried. "Shit, ya!"

Odin's good eye, his left eye, operated like a magic telescope, quickly pulling George's worried face out of the cleanup room and toward Odin as if the man were on wheels. Then that eye closed, too.

"Odin!" George cried. "Oh, man!"

Odin felt George pull his hands from his right eye. He smelled the dish soap on the man's arms and the sweet grease residue on his fingers. George's hands were remarkably soft and strong. They held Odin's fingers down, then pushed his body a few steps backwards into a chair.

"What's going on?" Odin heard Kryzinski ask. Then: "Oh, shit, I'll get Cushing."

Menker came, then Kowalski, then Burke, all exclaiming at first, then rushing over. When Odin managed to open his left eye for a moment, he saw a circle of faces, most prominently George's, which gazed back worried, then quickly smiled.

"I'll call an ambulance," he heard Cushing say from across the room, his voice fading as he ran off.

"We got it now, Zapata," Burke said. "Thanks."

"I don't mind," George said, letting go of Odin's hands which snapped right back to his eye. "You see," George said.

"He's got to have someone hold his hands."

"We've got it under control," Burke said. "These things happen in this profession."

Odin let out a laugh that sounded like a screech and then everyone started yelling again. The sweet smell of George, close, insistent, made Odin dizzier.

"We oughta take a look at his eye," Kryzinski said.

"I'll do it," Menker said.

"Oh, no," Odin tried to say, but it came out as a croak.

"Leave it alone!" George said sharply. "Let the doctor. They'll be here soon."

Odin opened his left eye in time to see Menker's face pressed against his own. The man's broad nose and hairy nostrils filled his sight; he saw large pores, slick skin.

"Don't do it, Menker," George said.

Odin closed his eye. A sharp stick pressed down on whatever was caught under his right eyelid. It started as a slow prod, then the pain grew, a tearing, boiling again. Odin wrenched his hands free from George's grasp and slapped his palms to his eye.

"Aaah," he said, feeling his mouth drop open, aghast at the pain's strength. His whole body rocked far forward on the chair then suddenly bucked backwards. His head hit the wall with a crack. Bonehead, Odin had time to think, and then he was out.

Odin came to in the soft white—from lights, window shades, sheets, godawful butt-baring gown—of the hospital. Against the white, a concerned face and a head of black hair. George, smiling.

"Finally," George said, breathing out.

Odin gingerly touched his right eye where it lay moving, grating, it seemed, under a pile of cotton gauze. George sat framed in the good eye. The side and tip of Odin's broad nose protruded into the picture; this view of the world was precarious, as if this eye, too, would close down like the last shot in those cartoons when the screen screws shut to black around the character's head.

Odin closed his left eye and then, curiously, the pain started. He winced. "Cripes," he said, and gasped.

"Keep them both closed, Odin," George said. "The doctor said not to do too much and wear out the other one. Cushing called your sisters," George added. "He said to tell you."

Odin groaned, shifted in the bed. "I gotta see," he said. "I gotta look over things."

"What you have to do now is relax," George said. "I have the whole report. I wrote everything down." Odin heard paper rustling.

"It's like a peeled grape, your eye," George said.

"A what?"

"A grape, peeled. That's what the doctor said. Some covering got scraped away, I don't know what it's called."

"I thought you wrote it down."

"I did, but it was a long name. The whole thing is sore and open, and you have to wear a bandage and then a patch."

"A patch! Like a pirate, you mean?"

"Like a Viking at sea," George said. "Ha, ha."

"What was it?" Odin asked. "In my eye."

"A bone fragment," George said. "A tiny piece, the doctor said, but really sharp."

"Jeez."

"I know. Some butcher you are."

George was silent, waiting, Odin knew, for him to laugh. But he couldn't even think of it now—the cleaver, the bone fragment like a shooting star, the eye, a red, pulpy grape. Those red grapes of summer, perfect globes, with the hard seeds to spit, a cluster of them he saw once next to a pork chop on a plate in a photograph on a work calendar. The real astonishing event, the miracle, was the fact that he was here, anywhere, with George in close proximity. He liked the idea of the two of them together constructing the story of his injury.

"How'd I get here?" Odin asked. He wanted to figure out where George came in.

"In the ambulance, brother," George said. "You were in no shape to drive, being knocked out and all. Oh," he added, paper rustling. "You have a contusion on your head. A bump."

"No kidding," Odin said. He opened his eye. The tip of his nose obscured one side of George's smooth brow. He moved his head slightly, but there was no way to get his own features completely out of the picture. George looked at him with an exaggerated expression: a big grin and eyebrows raised as if he were trying to get a baby to smile.

"How'd you manage it?" Odin whispered.

George quickly looked away. "Manage?" he asked.

"You know what I'm saying," Odin whispered. Almost the last thing he'd seen: George in his white shirt, sleeves up, lap hard against the steel sink, the grease to his elbows. He felt a stirring again, then water in his eyes that sent him down a hot chute of pain. "Yaaa," he said, closing his eye.

"All right," George said quietly, "don't get excited."

"Somebody ought to," Odin said.

No one else could go, apparently. Kryzinski was next in command, so he had to stay and then have at least two others with him, union rules, then Burke was off his shift and had to go home because he'd made some promises about something else, and of course Cushing couldn't leave, and Forrest, George's assistant in Produce was there, so, well, in short, George finally confessed, he had volunteered.

Odin smiled at George, a painful grimace he could feel open the whole front of his face, like a dog grinning. "All the attention's appreciated," he said, opening his eye.

"It's a hospital," George said. He was still smiling at Odin in that extreme way, as if he were modeling happiness.

"Still. The personal."

"Yes," George said. He looked toward the closed blinds, a sheet of splintered white.

"You ever been married?" Odin asked suddenly.

George looked back, unsmiling. "Why?" he asked.

Odin laughed. "I don't know," he said. "Some fellows do it, you know."

"No, why do you ask?"

"It's a question, George, that's all," Odin said. "I'm just making conversation."

"No, you're not. How old do you think I am, Odin?"

"My age."

"Which is," George said.

"Forty about."

"Okay," George said. "Give me ten guys' hands raised and I'll tell you how many times I've been asked if I was married."

"And the answer is," Odin said.

"Never," George said. "Okay?"

"Don't get mad. Do you know who you're talking to here?"

"Maybe. Another man who was never married."

"That's right," Odin said. With his eye closed, he could place George and himself in any setting. Now they were in Odin's living room, in the La-Z-Boys, drinking beers and sidling up closer to the truth and to each other. If Odin stopped now—and he could, having the power to turn the conversation around so that he and George said nothing to each other–he wouldn't have risked a thing and his life could go stumbling along as it always had. If he told George the truth and George bolted, what had he lost? Who would listen to George at work, assuming he even told anyone? Who would believe that a man like Odin could be a fairy? No one. This was the real power Odin's secret had: It didn't fit. He had a disguise, skin over skin. He had fashioned a life so impenetrable and unreadable on the outside that the truth about himself became an almost irrelevant weakness.

"Ask me," Odin said, "what I was thinking before I hurt my eye."

"Okay," George said. He sighed.

"I was watching you wash your hands at the sink," Odin said.

"No wonder you hurt yourself, not paying attention like that." George laughed nervously.

"And I was thinking about how much I'd like to help you," Odin continued.

"Help me what?" George said quietly.

"Help you there, in the water," Odin said.

He opened his eye. George sat stiff, silent, but he looked straight at Odin. Magic words, Odin thought.

"Wash you," Odin said.

"Me," George whispered.

"That's right," Odin said. "Now tell me I'm wrong here."

"About what?" George asked.

"Tell me I've scared you here," Odin said.

"No, I'm not scared. Of what?"

"You're lying," Odin whispered fiercely. He saw red blood, felt red pain, heard George and himself and the room fall under a crashing wave of red. The color of alarm. "I just scared the shit out of you, George," he said loudly.

George looked around the hospital room, though there was nothing to see. That's the whole point of these places, Odin wanted to say, they give you nothing to concentrate on but the sick person. Look at me: I'm the only thing going in the room. Finally, George's eyes returned to Odin in a softened face.

"Odin," George began, "tell me what good it would do if I told the truth? What if I agree to be frightened? Or worse, what if I wish for something, too?"

Odin caught his breath. He closed his eye. In the dark, safe behind his eyelids, he saw long, brown fingers move across his back, a narrow kneecap, a sleek black head under his own huge hands. "Go ahead and wish," he whispered to George.

"I must say something to you, Odin," George said after a moment. "You are not a very worldly man."

"What do you mean?" Odin asked. What had he missed in the magazines? At the bookstore?

"Don't you know the consequences of what we're talking about?"

"Consequences?" Odin asked. He felt bigger, stupider, a monster trapped in a baby's crib.

"Laws!" George was nearly shouting. "Why do you think we wait until now, alone in a sick room, of all places, to talk about this?"

Odin exhaled slowly. Laws. What was illegal about feeling virtuous? And happy? This was a pure, man-only story, like a war movie, John Wayne the hero maybe, head wrapped in bandages and tended by his comrade fresh from the battle. Bombs all around. Why not? Odin wanted George's own healing hands on him; he wanted the man's strong fingers, wiry arms—he'd seen them now—his hot breath, cotton shirt permeated with that orchard smell, smothered fruit. At one of Odin's father's farms there had been a small collection of apple trees, far beyond the two big cow pastures. Odin and his friend Norman sat under a tree one day and stuffed themselves with apples, and then there'd been a tussle between the two of them, both of them joking, rolling under the tree, crushing the rotten apples, juice on their skin and hair. Like he was playing, testing, or maybe he made a mistake, Norman had moved his knee up into Odin's crotch and Odin did the same. They rolled for a while like that, pushed, breathless, then broke apart laughing, said good-bye, and went opposite ways home, though they lived on adjacent farms.

"Laws," Odin said, disgusted. "I know what laws you're referring to. But people have these friendships in private. We're not out on the street."

"We have families, Odin. They expect certain things from us. Or don't expect others. I've thought about this for a long time. There are ways to do things, and ways not. How to live, who to be. And you aren't going to find many people who include us."

"Awww," Odin groaned. He wrinkled his brow, sending stabs of pain through his eyes. "Aren't you tired of this, George? You especially?" His voice rose. "Be like us or don't be anything, that's what my sisters and their husbands say, but where does this leave someone who can't help it? Like us? We might as well not have been born."

"People can change themselves," George said quietly. "Keep things to themselves."

"I understand that," Odin said forcefully. His voice filled the hospital room; he felt a pain in the back of his head. "You think I don't know that?" he asked. "I've led a quiet life all these years. No one. Nobody." His face grew hot, sweaty. This was grim labor, justifying yourself.

"There must have been someone," George said. "Otherwise how would you know about yourself?"

"There were a couple," Odin said.

"When?" George asked quickly.

"The army," Odin said. "And a few times by accident, I guess you'd call it. But I don't like it that way, by accident."

"I had a friend in high school," George said dreamily. "A boy in my class. We got caught by a teacher but she kept it quiet."

George's soft voice brushed Odin like kissing. "Oh-oh," Odin whispered. He opened his eye. George was looking right at him, Odin of the busted eye, flushed face, and gargantuan dimensions. "Well, you're an older fellow now," Odin said.

"Yes, I am," George said.

Just then the door flew open and in marched the sisters, cooing and exclaiming all at once and descending on Odin's bed like birds at a feeder. He saw shopping bags, smelled turkey.

"Our baby brother!" Sonja said, gently kissing Odin's forehead.

"And your eye!" Lillian cried. "The most delicate part of a man." She began kneading the pillow under Odin's head until he cried out in pain.

Odin looked beseechingly after George, who was slinking away. "George!" he called.

George stopped, stared, as the sisters turned to see him for the first time. Then he bolted out the door.

"Who the heck was *that* guy?" Alma asked as she began rummaging through the drawers in Odin's nightstand.

"Yo-ho-ho!" the four black stock boys called when they saw Odin in the break room a week later.

"Odin, my man," one boy, Kevin, said. "You been on the high seas?"

"Aw, come on, now," Odin said, blushing. He lumbered over to the refrigerator with his lunch bag, tripping on the leg of a chair as he went. He still hadn't adjusted to the eye patch. He bumped his head on the doorjamb when he turned into a room, carved up one side of his face when he shaved, ran stop signs. The patch even got him into trouble with his family. His sisters had come over every day after he got home from the hospital, to make him food and to clean. They ambushed him nonstop, sliding up on his right side to plant kisses on his head and to slip plates of meatloaf and potatoes under his face. All he wanted now, though, was to see George again. That would be a fine thing, he thought, as he threw his lunch into the break room refrigerator, to have George's profile, black mole on his cheek like a period ending a long sentence, glide out of the dark right side of the screen on which Odin's world played and move into the light of his good eye.

But instead he got the other meat cutters, George being off until the afternoon, who greeted him with backslaps and faked punches to the stomach.

"You old Viking," Kowalski said. "Now you really look the part."

"The man of mystery," Burke said. "You know, Vike, the ladies will love this."

Menker said, "They'll think he's that Arrow shirt guy like in the magazines until they really get a look at him."

Everyone laughed. Odin's face burned, his right eye twitched until he gasped. "Anything I should know about?" he asked, breathless.

"Naw," Kryzinski said. He had on his half glasses because he'd been reading the order sheet but also, Odin knew, to show that he had been in charge and had taken his job seriously. "Nothing except that Pavel's a nut case," Kryzinski said.

"So what else is new?" Menker whispered to the group.

"I think it's that damn gun," Burke said.

"Oh, now he's not still bringing that around, is he?" Odin asked.

"Every day," Kowalski said, nodding.

"Vike," Kryzinski said, "the man's doing his work, I'm not saying otherwise, but he's more quiet lately and he snaps at the stock boys. Hardly talks to us."

"He's always been weird," Burke said.

"This doesn't sound like reasons to worry," Odin said. "A man's allowed his differences."

"Mmmno, it's not the same," Kryzinski said, shaking his head. "Couple of days ago a Chinese lady come up to the counter and what does Pavel do? He turns his back and won't wait on her."

"She's saying, ''Scuse me, 'scuse me,'" Menker said, adopting a falsetto, "but Pavel, he doesn't even look."

"I talked to him later, Vike," Kryzinski said. "I told him you got to wait on everybody, regardless. You want to know what he said?"

"I don't think I do," Odin said. He closed his good eye to rest it, and to prepare it for a blow.

"He said, 'Let the pigs eat dirt,'" Kryzinski reported.

"Cripes," Odin said, and sighed.

"Then he goes right past me," Burke says, "I was there at the time—pushes right on by and out the door, gone for the day. AWOL. Not a word."

"I put him on half time this week," Kryzinski said. He looked at his watch. "He'll be in this afternoon."

"Well," Odin said, walking off to get his apron and get to work, "we'll keep an eye on him."

"That's it?" Kryzinski called after him.

"That's it!" Odin yelled back. They wanted a big deal, Odin thought; they wanted to bring Odin back to work with a crisis and in the meantime they wanted to push a guy out. Let Pavel fight on his own. Odin had his own battles with George and himself.

He did the easier things all day: He finished up the ordering, wrapped a lot of steaks and chops, put it all out in the cases, and he found he had to take quite a few breaks. It wasn't as if his body were tired, but rather his mind. Or his heart. It had slowed to maintenance level since his aborted talk with George.

He'd heard from him two or three times while he was home recovering, but they'd never had a satisfactory conversation, what with his sisters always hovering and his eye poking him in the head with pain. He couldn't tell how much George wanted to talk to him, or how much was just politeness. But at least he stayed in contact. Now, as Odin sat in the busted armchair in the break room and held his head, he could barely remember George's face; he could only imagine the man, recreate him as he hoped he would be, and he realized with a long, slow twinge in his gut that imagining George might be the closest he'd come to knowing him. Was the idea so outrageous, the idea of him and George, that it could never be real? Too dangerous was more like it, like his family's reaction to the movie on TV the other night in which a Mexican man romanced a white woman. They couldn't even tell Odin what they were so mad about, only that it was unthinkable, brown hand on white body; there weren't any words to describe such an abomination. So how could there possibly be words for Odin and George? Only pictures, the kind that Lancelot's Books sold, and pictures didn't tell the whole story, not by a longshot. Odin rolled his head back and forth in his palms.

Pavel burst into the break room muttering and slamming around. Odin didn't look up. Through his good eye, he saw Pavel's worn Hush Puppies stomp by on his way to the refrigerator. The gym bag also swung into view.

"Aren't you going to say hello, Pavel?" Odin asked, raising his head.

Pavel glanced at him and burst out laughing. "Oh, Vike, you're showboatin'," he said.

Odin laughed uncertainly.

"Or else it's Fearless Leader with half sight," Pavel added.

"The last thing, I guess," Odin said.

Pavel stood still in the middle of the room. "Kryzinski put me on half days," he said. "What do you think of that?"

Odin shrugged. "I think it's up to Kryzinski," he said slowly.

Pavel took a deep breath. "Well, I think that's chicken shit, Vike."

"Okay," Odin said. He raised his hands, then let them drop onto the arms of the chair.

Pavel shook his head. "High and mighty," he muttered, "high and mighty." He left the break room, taking his gym bag with him.

When George came in to work a few hours later, he leaned down past the edge of the last aisle and waved to Odin, then popped back to work before he could possibly have noticed Odin's big smile and friendly wave. As if nothing had happened, as if nothing had been said in the hospital. Not only were there no words for what George and Odin might have had, now there was nothing to name.

Odin went glumly about his business, cleaning up the cutting surfaces, figuring the schedule for next month, catching up with Cushing in a desultory way, Odin half in and half out of the office cage, his good eye firm on the ever-so-slightly moving rollers of the manager's chair. When Odin left at five-thirty from the service door, it had started to snow big, fat flakes that looked like the lint that spit out of the dryer hose on the side of his house. The snow provided a speckled backdrop for Pavel jiggling the key in the door lock of his Monte Carlo, and for Kevin, the stock boy, who sat sprawled on the whitening concrete next to the car, blood from his lip streaking the front of his white shirt crimson.

"Pavel!" Odin cried, starting down the stairs next to the loading dock.

"Son of a bitch!" Kevin screamed, trying to stand.

Pavel jammed another key into the lock.

"Son of a bitch hit me, tried to kill me," Kevin said, struggling to rise. He grabbed the side mirror of Pavel's car.

"Get your dirty, thieving hands off my car," Pavel said slowly. He stopped working the lock, put down his gym bag, and began to unzip it.

"No!" Odin cried, rushing Pavel and flattening him against the side of the car.

Kevin scrambled to his feet and began punching around Odin's back, trying to connect with Pavel. "Asshole son of a bitch!" Kevin cried. "Bohunk ofay," he added, spinning away from the car.

"What happened?" Odin asked, breathing into Pavel's face. One of Pavel's pale, no-color eyes turned away from Odin's gaze. His chin was covered in blond and red stubble, his breath sour and flat.

"Little shit tried to steal my car," Pavel said, struggling.

"Steal your car!" Kevin screamed, rushing for Pavel again. He pressed up against Odin's back for a moment. "I was picking up my goddamn wallet!" he yelled at Odin's neck. "That I dropped! By the car! And this motherfucker hits me before I even know he's there! Son of a bitch!" He spun away again.

Pavel's eye swung back into Odin's view. "Miserable nigger thief," he said matter-of-factly. Odin winced. His injured eye beat like a drum in his head.

"That's it!" Kevin yelled. But instead of trying to jump Pavel again, he ran off through the parking lot and down the sidewalk, his shoes slapping up slush. Odin leaped off Pavel.

The man stayed flattened against the side of the car, breathing hard, his face turned away from Odin. "You going to call the cops?" Pavel asked quietly, shifting his eyes to the sky, which leaked snow.

"You know what I have to do," Odin said sadly. He watched Pavel reach for the handle of his gym bag, but he didn't stop him.

"You're as bad as any of them," Pavel said, jerking his head in the direction Kevin had run. He swung the gym bag with one hand and fingered his keys with the other, separating them slowly, looking for the right one. He had become way too calm, way too quickly, Odin thought.

"You know that?" Pavel asked, looking up at Odin. "You're as bad as any of them."

"Forget about all that noise," Odin said. "You put yourself in a place now where you're in trouble, and for what?"

"Some guys don't see where the world's going," Pavel said. "I feel sorry for you."

"Feel sorry for yourself, Pavel," Odin said. "I've gotta fire you."

"Nigger-lover," Pavel said calmly, finding the key and sticking it in the lock. "Chink-lover," he said, opening the car door. "Jew-lover," Pavel said. "Spic-lover."

"Keep going, Pavel," Odin said. "All the way home, calm, no trouble." He could feel each heartbeat in the center of his damaged eye.

Pavel slammed the car door and started the engine. Then he

drove slowly out of the parking lot, the roof of his car carrying an undisturbed mat of white flakes.

The opinion was divided, in the same way the public weighs in on a high-profile criminal trial. Odin's family and the rest of the guys in Meat thought he'd been too hasty about Pavel. Poor guy, they thought; provoked by the stock boy, they figured. Mr. Cushing said what Odin had done was okay, though he wished there'd been time to consult about it first, it being Christmastime, too, but he could see how with the gun and all—if there was a gun, there being no proof on that day that there actually was one—that Odin had to think of safety first, so, sure, that was the right thing, he (Cushing) just hoped he wouldn't hear from the union was all. Kevin quit the next day, telling Cushing he figured he'd be fired anyway, and not getting an answer from the manager (according to Cushing), he left his stock apron and took his pay for the week. The other stock boys, though, the other black kids, they seemed to really think about Odin and what he'd done. Odin figured they were smart enough to see that he didn't fire Pavel just for Kevin's sake, that Kevin was just a symptom of the real cause of Pavel's demise, but all the same Odin felt the boys watching him, reading him in a new way. What he'd done was take the bloody face of Kevin as seriously as he would take the bloody face of Kryzinski or Menker, or any other white worker.

But George, whose opinion mattered most to Odin, was silent. He came to work, of course, and he smiled, he waved, even exchanged a few pleasantries with Odin about his healing eyeball, but not a word did he utter about Pavel's firing and, as Odin saw it, Odin's own bravery.

In the weeks following, while they looked for a new guy to replace Pavel, Odin took on some extra hours, so he was around more to see when George came in, when he left, what his face looked like each day. It was the dead time right after

New Year's, so there wasn't much call for party food or roasts for family gatherings, just regular ladies again, their kids stuffed into snowsuits like sausage into casings, noses red from the cold. Every day George came in to work slapping his hands to warm them and rubbing the circulation back into his thighs, the latter movement Odin wished he could keep himself from watching.

Odin stayed late one night so he could take his time cleaning up and think about how to handle George. After scrubbing down the tables and the sinks and mopping the floor, Odin sat on a high stool in the cutting room with a torn piece of butcher paper and the stub of grease pencil he kept behind his ear. A note might do it: friendly, cheerful, just a casual thing.

"Dear George," he began.

He tore another piece of paper off of the big roll.

> George—
> Hey, how are you? How about let's have a beer sometime, maybe soon? I really never said "thank you" for going with me to the hospital. I'm much better now. Isn't it slow what with the holidays over and all? When you come in tomorrow come on over and tell me if you want to have a beer sometime, maybe soon. I'll be the guy behind the Meat Counter with the bum eye—ha-ha. I'm putting this note in your locker.
>
> —Odin

The next day Odin waited. He watched George bustle for an hour over at the end of the produce section setting up a pyramid of Florida grapefruit, but the man never looked his way. At his lunch break, Odin made a point of picking through the pears, glancing over periodically to try to catch George's eye. Nothing. Odin ate his lunch in silence surrounded by the rest of the Meat guys who were still chewing over Pavel's craziness and his firing. No one had heard from him, though

Menker, and then Burke, swore they had seen Pavel's Monte Carlo prowling the parking lot after work the week before. At one point a couple of the black stock boys came in and Menker and Burke shut up. The boys crossed the break room to get RCs out of the machine, all the while looking at Odin quietly munching away at his Braunschweiger on rye and trying to stay out of things.

Later that afternoon, Odin did a stint in the meat locker. Product had come up missing over the past month or so: a carton of sirloin, one of pork chops, about thirty pounds of ground beef. Odin had discovered the discrepancies after his return from the hospital. Since the incident with Pavel he figured that the thefts were just part of the guy's crazy behavior. Now Odin had to do a surface reinventory of the whole locker. Who knew how much was missing? He put on his sheepskin gloves and his quilted hunting cap but otherwise he wore his work clothes and his ever present apron stained with rust-colored blood.

All he thought about as he counted, moved, and marked down product was George. George laughing at a joke as he leaned toward Odin over the chicken display; George smiling when he saw Odin galumph into Produce and start examining broccoli; George building castles of apples, lemons, even mangoes; George at his sink, his sleeves rolled up, hips pressed to the metal basin. George cinching his apron around his narrow waist, ready for work. George in Lancelot's bookstore, knocking over racks of books and magazines to get at Odin. George over and under him, finally. Ooof, what an idiot, Odin thought, counting out cartons of sirloin and packages of chops and ground beef, I'm like a fool waiting for a prom date, like a groom at the altar. Lovesick. He tore off his gloves and moved the frozen boxes with his bare hands, letting his skin stick to the frost-covered cardboard. His breath came in great clouds. Idiot, idiot, he chanted to himself. It wasn't the visions he had of George that humiliated him, it was the fact that he let himself have the visions in the first place. He had hope, the most persistent of all his wasted desires.

He worked furiously. His eye throbbed, but not from his exertions. After a while, after he began sniffling violently, he realized that he was crying. Tears stung his injured eye and that made more come fiercer, faster. He stopped working. The frigid air eventually slowed his crying, but not his devastation. What kind of man cries? Odin remembered his father asking him when he was a boy. No man I know, his father had said, not unkindly, handing Odin a bandanna and turning away. That was right after Odin's best friend, Norman, had left town, and Odin's heart had been enveloped by fear, love, and embarrassment. Now he would just have to harden up, he thought, restacking the boxes he'd just checked. Nothing but ice and snow in the heart.

The freezer door opened and a cloud of vapor sucked out. George entered the meat locker through the fog already shivering, holding his narrow arms in their rolled-up sleeves, the sweet scent of his green apron snaking toward Odin through the rolling air.

"It's bright in here," George said, squinting.

"It's all the white," Odin said. "The paper and boxes and walls and all that. You're not dressed right," he added, turning back to his task.

"I wasn't planning a trip in here," George said. "It just happened."

"Yeah?" Odin asked.

"I got your note, Odin," George said.

"I put it in there a while ago," Odin said, pretending to be busy. He circled the meat locker, moving boxes and packages this way and that.

"Only yesterday," George said. He paused. "I'm sorry, Odin," he added.

"For what?"

"For not being the kind of friend you want." George stood

in front of Odin, stopping him on his circuit of the meat locker.

Odin looked George square in the face. The man was pale, shivering. Chicken, Odin thought, and then he noticed that he was trembling also. "You're a liar," Odin said to George.

"I beg your pardon?" George asked.

"I don't think for one minute that you're not that kind of guy," Odin said. The cold closed over him, body and mind. "You all but said it before, and I don't make mistakes about that anyway."

"I didn't say I wasn't that kind of friend," George said. "I said that I couldn't *be* the kind of guy you mean. I couldn't act that way."

"I can see if you say you can't be with *me*," Odin said. "But you can't say you aren't that way at all, that's the lie. Maybe you need some reminding about how you really feel. Think of it that way," he added hopefully. "I'm a reminder. A big reminder."

"You can feel things in your inside," George said, shaking his head, "but you can keep a different face for the outside. Don't tell me you don't know about that."

"Is it because you're Mexican?" Odin asked, thinking out loud and instantly regretting it. He felt a kind of prickly frost forming on his upper lip as he breathed in and out.

"What does that have to do with anything?" George asked, his voice rising.

"I don't know," Odin said. "I thought maybe religion, or your family, or something. Maybe you feel there are different rules for you."

George stared at Odin, an expression of wonder and anger on his face. He breathed out a few cloudy breaths. "Odin," he finally said, "what you don't know about the world is truly amazing to me sometimes."

Odin found this comment hopeful. He smiled.

But George remained stern. "I'm going now, Odin," he said. "And I'm sorry."

"Yes, you are," Odin said. He put on his sheepskin gloves and bent to pick up a box, but instead he straightened up and grabbed George's face.

George backed up, trying to free himself, but Odin refused to let go. "Ooof!" George cried, tripping over a box. "Odin!"

And there commenced a dance of sorts, Odin leading, pushing George, George trying unsuccessfully to swing away. Odin pushed at George's body as if he were a boy again, fighting, or pretending to fight, so he could get contact with some other boy's body. He pressed against George as they both moved around the freezer, bumping George into boxes and carts, sliding his hands over George's back, buttocks, the nape of his neck, when he could. He tried to kiss George, but each time George jerked his head away at the last second. Odin was breathless, but not from physical work; this was labor of the head, heart, and eye. At one point, Odin thought he could see in stereo again when he looked upon the full force of George's miserable, churning face set before him in the blank frostiness of the meat locker, so close was Odin for the first time to what he wanted.

George freed one arm from Odin's grasp and turned, curving himself for a moment into Odin's arms, breathing heavily. "Stop it!" he cried after a pause, then he resumed struggling.

Odin finally pressed his face against George's cheek and shoved the two of them toward some boxes, where they collapsed.

"All right, all right," Odin said, releasing George and rising. He clapped his gloved hands a few times.

"How is this going to help?" George asked from the floor, gasping.

"It doesn't help," Odin replied. "Nothing helps, George, if you're going to see things the way you do."

Odin pulled George up from the floor, grasped the back of his head with one hand, and kissed him solidly on the mouth.

George started to twist away, but then, it seemed to Odin, he stopped fighting.

"There," Odin said, stepping away.

George swallowed. "Odin," he whispered.

Odin thought for a moment that George moved toward him, or that he almost smiled. But George just stared at Odin with his wet eyes, gestured weakly, then turned and fled the meat locker, disturbing a cloud of vapor as he opened the door.

Odin picked up two boxes from the floor and threw each one hard against the wall of the freezer. They broke open, spilling lamb shanks and chicken parts in a frozen jumble on the floor.

When Odin stopped at a traffic light that night, a woman in the car next to him cringed when he glanced over at her. He looked in the rearview mirror: a shock of blond hair straight up over his forehead, the rest fluffed above his ears, his eye patch a bit askew so that part of his pink eyelid was showing. This creature is what I'm left with, he thought. Pawing, grunting, desperate, just like an animal. He teetered on the edge of self-disgust, but came back. No. Whether through accidents or planned conquests, he was not the only man who felt this way. George was flat wrong. There were the men who made the magazines he read, there were the accidental men, and there were other men like George. And like Odin. Others. You had to have the men already in order to make the places for them to go, the bookstores, the special streets. Customers created demand. Otherwise all these men would be totally invisible, cowering. And even tonight Odin had seen George large as life, sitting stock still in his car in the Jewel parking lot, the motor running, watching Odin with only his eyes as he swerved angrily onto North Avenue. Now Odin was about to turn into the alley behind Potomac when he swerved again and headed toward Chicago Avenue and downtown.

The air was colder downtown, and the wind more fierce, catching Odin in a swirling gust as he got out of his car on Rush Street. Beer signs lit up the windows of bars and restaurants, sailors with women strolled by, looking drunk or drugged, their faces pale white, shaded, and mahogany under the streetlights. The meaning of a crowd. The *Tribune* often called this life, all the electric bulbs and shadows and creeping men and women around Rush Street, "the underworld." Crime, they meant, drugs and bad living, and sex. Sex had its own neighborhood. Any sex that married people couldn't get at home you could find around here. Odin turned onto a side street, dim and dirty. Paper blew about his feet.

Three young men in tight pants leaned against the front of a corner grocery. Odin felt their eyes follow him as he walked past. At least he looked at home down here: wild hair, green work pants, soiled plaid shirt, ratty quilted jacket, and the eye patch to top it off. A renegade on the outside now. He half hoped one of the slim boys would follow him.

A feeling came back to him as he strode down the sidewalk, a memory that was so mangled and flattened that it entered his consciousness abruptly, like a piece of blowing trash scaring him out of the corner of his good eye. During the war, on leave in Tokyo, he'd had occasion to wander some other dark streets one night. Then he wasn't alone. Right away, a Japanese man had followed him, young—Odin's age then—in a threadbare jacket and a touring cap. When Odin stopped, the man behind him stopped. And when Odin ducked into an alley, the sounds of nightclubs and rowdy bars all around him, the man had slipped in to face Odin, his hands already searching Odin's body. When he saw the uniform under Odin's coat, the man stopped suddenly and pulled away, but Odin grabbed him back. He had spirit then, Odin now thought, real guts, brought on not by the war but by the fact that he was in a foreign country. With foreigners. Who would ever know? He had grabbed the man back.

Men did look at him now, tonight, young and old men; he tried with his one eye to really see them all, faces and bodies abloom with idiosyncrasies: a fringe of hair around a narrow head; a needle nose; enormous brown eyes in a face that looked plum-colored in the light and shadows of the street. All of them, Odin included, moving without a break. This was lust in motion; only the right signal from someone and a shadowy place to meet allowed the men to stop. Everything had to be hidden, especially the fact that you wanted one another in the first place.

Odin realized that the only way he could venture here was to put George out of his mind. He stopped looking at faces then and instead noticed the muscular thighs of two sailors going by. A young man waited to cross the street in an Eisenhower jacket and jeans so tight they squeezed his buttocks. Another man, his hands in his trouser pockets, discreetly fondled himself as he walked. Odin stopped in front of a coffee shop to catch his breath. This was like one of those police shows. The underbelly of the city, home of the vice squad. You never knew who was looking. Two cops could do it, keys, handcuffs jingling as they moved together. The stick of a badge come loose.

"Excuse me," a voice next to Odin said.

Odin turned to see a short, redheaded man of about thirty who smiled up at him, blinking watery blue eyes. Toggle coat and blue jeans and loafers and a button-down shirt. He looked like a college kid who got held back. And shaky hands, too, as the guy pinched a battered cigarette in one and with the other pointed to the tip.

Odin patted his pockets as he stared at the man. "Sorry," he said, moving forward a step. It was time to use his size to his advantage. If he was a man whose body said look at me, then let them look up close.

"Maybe there's some matches in there," Odin said. He jerked his thumb toward the restaurant.

"No, that's okay," the man said, looking dejected. He put

the cigarette in his coat pocket. "It's not good for me anyway."

"Right," Odin said. He turned back to the street.

And there they stood. In Lancelot's you had the protection of the four walls and the other guys like yourself, but here, even on the sinful streets of Chicago, you had to watch. You never knew who was looking. Two teenage girls in jeans and pea coats stopped at a phone booth and checked the coin return. A half block down at the intersection a police car cruised by, silent, its light flashing.

"I better go," Odin finally said. He began to walk, setting off at a jaunty gait as if he were out for a Sunday stroll.

He heard the man coughing behind him, then his footsteps in the next moment, quick behind the sound of Odin's slower strides. He thought he caught a smile from another young man coming his way swathed in a parka and smoking a cigar.

Odin walked for two blocks, slowing up and then racing, just to make sure of the man behind him. Simon says. Odin's stomach and heart seemed to rise, his eye relax. This was how you were always supposed to feel, excited, full of anticipation. This was what came from making the world bend in your direction. He could already imagine his arm around the man's waist.

Odin ducked into an alley, his heart floating. There was a weak light bulb in a cage hanging over the back door of a business, but otherwise the space was dark. Trash cans and flattened boxes lined the alley. There was no one in sight, not even a garbage picker or a drunk, not another queer.

Odin headed down the alley, slowing until he was sure he heard the man's footsteps. Then he stopped, hidden, beside a tall Dumpster.

There was no wind in the alley, just the sound of it blowing fiercely by on the street. An odor of urine drifted up from the pavement, and a smell of stale food and dirty clothing came from the Dumpster, like the smell in an old person's home.

Odin waited against the wall, his hands in the pockets of his quilted jacket. His injured eye felt loose in his head, as if in healing it would gradually leave his body. He listened, but all he heard now was muffled noise from the building behind him, the whine of the wind, and something scuttling through paper a few feet away.

Then the redheaded man was in front of Odin and without hesitating he threw himself forward onto Odin's chest. Odin saw half of him, a split screen. The man's coat was open, his belt buckle undone, his hands working at Odin's zipper.

"Come on, now," Odin whispered. "Hold on." He took his hands out of his pockets to help the man.

Like a kid concentrating on tying his shoelaces, Odin thought, watching the top of the man's red head bobbing against his chest. Hard to be adult about all this secret work. That's how you stayed cowed, a case of arrested development, though the rest of the population took the act seriously enough to put the handcuffs on men like them.

"There," the man finally whispered. He thrust in his hand.

"Ya," Odin cried, then grabbed the man's curly hair.

The man pulled slowly with one hand and pressed the palm of the other against the side of the building next to Odin's shoulder, positioning himself. He rested his cheek against Odin's shirt.

Glass broke at the mouth of the alley, then Odin heard laughter, then a shout. He pulled up the man's head by his hair. The man's hand moved faster.

"Stop!" Odin whispered. "Shit, oh."

"Wait!" the man said.

"Somebody's here," Odin said. He gulped air through his teeth.

No!" the man said. He took his hand off the wall and grabbed Odin's hip. His head descended.

"Christ almighty," Odin muttered, pushing the man away. They'd get stuck, then caught, like two dogs locked together fucking in a farmyard. Odin quickly zipped up his pants, then his coat. The man stared at him from a few feet away. "Go!" Odin said. But the man just stood, pants unbuckled, his nostrils damp. He sniffed.

"I can tell you what's coming," Odin said, shoving his hands in his pockets. His crotch pained him. The man stared, studying Odin's face as if memorizing him. Odin tried to laugh, looked to the street, looked back at the man.

"Okay," Odin said, "suit yourself." He took off.

Just as he got to the street, two drunks reeled into the alley, muttering and shoving each other.

"Hey!" one drunk said to Odin. He carried a paper bag in his fist. Odin could hear broken glass tinkling inside. "What's your problem?" the guy asked. Half of the man's head was shaved, and he had a long line of stitches on the side of his skull, terminating just over his ear. He thrust the paper bag in Odin's direction.

"He don't want any!" the other drunk cried, pulling at his friend's sleeve. Stuffing protruded from a tear across the front of his nylon coat, the cloth held together with a diaper pin.

Odin ran off. "Stay loose!" shaved head yelled after him. Both men laughed.

Everything hurt on Odin: his eye, his heart, his crotch. His lungs. It had been so long since he had run full speed. After a block or so he developed a rhythm to his strides that ate through the pain. People jerked their heads to see him race by. Running to or running from? they probably thought. Was he really going to stop the redheaded man back there? Could he stop him? And next time, he knew, he wouldn't even consider it. Once you got a taste of it this way, illicit, maybe you couldn't have a man any other way. There was George's face behind Odin's two eyes, healthy and busted alike, George all over in him, washing the redhead away. He'd barely touched George, but even one kiss made all other men seem sour. Down one curb and up the next, not a foot out of step. Maybe this was George's way, the alley, and that's why he said no to Odin.

George could have a lock on secrets, for all Odin knew; he could be down any one of these streets clinched and rocking with another man.

Odin ran faster, raging down the street back to his car. He caught what he could out of his left eye, looking directly at everyone, regardless of who they were. Damn it all, he thought, holding a swift stare with a black man who winked back at him. Damn us all, if that's what it takes, or if that's what it means to be us. He glared unconsciously at a woman in a mangy fur coat and knit cap. She had vivid, moist eyes.

He tuned in his car radio to one of the rock and roll stations, anything to make noise and speed, and he cracked his window open despite the raw cold and the mean wind blowing in off the lake. Bodies bent against the weather flashed past him under streetlights. Coats, hats, gloves, jackets, dresses, brassieres, boxer shorts, panties—all these other bodies—flawed, fat and thin, hairy and smooth—so many layers covering up some imperfection, some other self, secrets surging through bloodstreams as if they were corpuscles.

Odin sped the car down side streets, took wrong turns, ran stop signs in neighborhoods that looked almost dead they were so decrepit. Every building housed someone like him. He thought of looking up George in the phone book and then bursting into his house, but the idea left him in a red flare of anger. Damn him, too, Odin thought. We'll all go together. If hell was full of people like himself, sitting on a system of secrets and the lies told to cover them up, then Odin preferred it to heaven.

He pulled into the alley behind his house and drove up to his garage door. Old newspaper tumbled and flattened against the cyclone fence around the backyard. The garage door rattled and banged like a roll of thunder when Odin raised it in the quiet alley. He got back in the car and drove it in, then turned off the engine, listening to the wind batter the beams and struts of the garage. A car drove slowly along the alley. The garage roof creaked. The scent of old wood, rope, and oiled machinery and gasoline filled the garage. The car ticked and slowed, as did Odin's heart. He was home. Inside he could be himself, outside he was either thrown in with the lost gods on Rush Street, desperate to use their unplumbed powers, or he had to stay at Jewel, in George's face every day, disguised as a righteous-looking mortal with a rotten soul. The difference between the two incarnations made for a powerless existence.

Odin got out of the car and hauled down the big garage door, then locked it. As he made his way toward the side door that led to the backyard, feeling along the roof of the car, he heard a movement. Mice, he thought, come in from the cold, but then a shape rose up from the other side of the car.

"Hello, Vike," the figure said.

It was dark, but Odin could make out a tall man with unruly hair. Then he saw the gun.

"Pavel," Odin said.

"It's me," Pavel replied happily.

"What are you doing in my garage?" Odin asked.

"That's not the question you should be asking, Vike," Pavel said.

Odin moved slightly toward the side door.

"You should be asking what I'm going to do with the gun," Pavel said. "Shouldn't you?"

Odin moved a few feet to his left again. "You don't work for me anymore, Frank," he said. Then he bolted.

"Hey!" Pavel cried.

They met up at the side door of the garage. "Stay there!" Pavel yelled.

"Pavel," Odin began, raising his hands.

"Shut up! Open the door!"

Odin obliged. He felt a hard shape on his back, snug up against a vertebra. He pitched forward at its pressure and began walking.

When they entered the backyard, Odin stopped. He looked

quickly to his left. He could run and try to take the cyclone fence along the alley. He didn't really think that Pavel would shoot him, but he didn't want him to try to miss and hit him anyway. Forward, he could go over the fence to the Montoyas', but their yard was emptier than Odin's, so Pavel would have a clear shot there, too. He lurched to the right, toward the back stairs. Violence begets violence: Did the pastor say that in catechism class? The lessons were all in Norwegian, an old language from an old man, intoned in the cold church basement, the pastor in a white robe like God himself.

"Move," Pavel said. "Into the house."

"Okay," Odin said.

Up the stoop, then unlock the back door, then into the dark kitchen where the refrigerator hummed and the air smelled close and warm from the furnace heat and eggs and bacon from breakfast. He'd left the dirty pan on the stove.

"Turn on the light," Pavel said.

The white of the appliances and of the enamel-topped table, even the sink filled with dishes, startled Odin. He turned to look at Pavel, but he couldn't see colors for some reason, only contrast, black to the white of the room. Pavel wore a black chamois shirt, a black quilted vest, and navy blue trousers. "You planned this," Odin said, surprised.

"Damn right," Pavel said.

The percolator stood on the counter; Odin knew it was half full. All he'd have to do was plug it in. He could pin some normal life on this chaos and the moment would fit into the rest of his life. Odin turned to ask Pavel if he wanted some coffee, or maybe a beer?, wasn't this all a joke?, but the face that met his good eye stopped him from speaking.

Pavel's already narrow head and face seemed even more drawn, as if he were subject to some perverse force of gravity that pulled in at his features. His auburn hair rose up in short, twisted waves from his head and his colorless eyes alighted everywhere but on Odin. Here was a selfish face, all its expressions created by only its owner's own scrambled ideas and images. There was no room for anyone else. Odin had to look away. He stared at a plate of his sister's stale Christmas cookies sitting on the counter under a sheet of wax paper. Was this the life written on that blank moon that hung over Chicago these days? If so, Odin resolved to stop looking to the sky for answers.

Pavel waved the gun back and forth, blinking rapidly, looking puzzled, as if he had neglected to plan beyond this point. He pointed the gun at Odin. "Go in the living room," he said.

Odin clomped heavily past the door to the attic stairs, through the tiny dining room, into the living room, worn chairs and sofa pointing toward the black eye of the big TV set.

"Turn on all the lights and close the curtains," Pavel said.

Odin stared out the picture window into the blustery dark as he pulled the cord on the drapes. Just one old car going by slowly, hesitating in front of his house, and the bare tree branches in the park pulsing shadows on the ground under the street lamps.

Pavel took them to each room then—the dining room, the bathroom, both bedrooms—and forced Odin to turn on all the lights and close the curtains in each one. Then he was at a loss again and stood in the tiny hallway between the two bedrooms and the bathroom pointing the gun at Odin in a relaxed way. Odin remembered Pavel standing in this same spot a few years ago during a work barbecue Odin had in the summer. Odin had come upon Pavel on his way to the bathroom. Surprised him, actually, as Pavel stood drinking a beer and smoking a cigarette in the dark hallway while he leaned, peering into Odin's bedroom.

"Shooting me isn't going to get your job back," Odin said. He adjusted his eye patch. "I'll be dead, or wounded, you in jail, and then where will you be?"

"My job?" Pavel asked. "So what about that now. But I need other things. You got any money, Vike?" He waved the gun.

"You wouldn't have to ask, Frank, if you hadn't been so stupid. But it comes down to you don't punch out other employees for nothing and carry a weapon everywhere. It's not good work practices."

"I don't care about that anymore," Pavel said, shaking his head. "I really don't. You can all rot in hell, all of you, kissing your black babies and counting your guilt money." He smiled. "Speaking of which," he said.

"This is stupid, Frank," Odin said. "Stupid and a waste of time."

"For God's sake, Vike," Pavel said, "wake up." He poked his gun toward Odin's chest. "We're in a war zone here. Chicago's going down on our heads, and you're going to be sorry, Odin, if you don't see it coming because it's going to catch you when you're not looking. You're in management, Christ almighty! You've got to take note of who's screwing who. I'm out money, the colored boys still got their jobs, and the likes of that Zapata is stocking Jewel full of God knows what kinds of shit Mexican food. I'm telling you, Vike, soon all of us'll be bringing guns to work."

Odin backed up into his bedroom and Pavel followed, stepping forward, the gun still drawn. Odin had in mind that he would slam the bedroom door in Pavel's face, but how this would stop a bullet he didn't know. That's how the Chicago police got those Black Panthers, bang bang through the wood while they were sleeping, or so said rumors. Odin's experience with defensive behavior took place daily, in slow, subtle increments, but now was different: Pavel had the power to break him open and leave him dead.

Odin backed up some more until he hit the bed. Pavel advanced.

"I bet you keep cash under that mattress," Pavel said. "That and God knows what else. Who's next after me? Kowalski? Or maybe Menker. They're the best, so you better get rid of them, too. Let the dummies run things so they can let other dummies in. Soon, Vike, there could be some colored girl taking over your job and living your picayune life just because someone said so, maybe you yourself. Special programs. A hand up. Who ever said someone deserved special for skin color? That's how Communism starts: be nice to everybody and nobody gets paid. The hell with that." Pavel waved the gun again.

Odin sat back on the bed as Pavel advanced. There was a commotion in the hallway, heavy footsteps, but Pavel seemed deaf, even smiling weakly at Odin. Then suddenly Pavel's eyes widened and he came plowing forward toward Odin, arms outstretched, only to collapse face first onto the floor in front of him. George—of all people!—clung to Pavel's back, pinning his arms to the carpet.

"What the hell!" Odin cried. "George!" It was Zapata all right, hair askew, coat falling off of his shoulders as he wrestled Pavel on the carpet. He was nearly tossed off his victim's bucking back.

"Hit him!" George yelled. "For God's sake, Odin, knock him out!"

Odin kicked the gun under the bed and then shoved George off Pavel's back, sitting astride him himself. Pavel groaned under Odin's weight. Odin laughed. The moment he'd seen George he had started grinning and now he couldn't stop.

"Fuck," Pavel muttered, his face against the carpet. "Jesus. Stupid shits."

"Good work, brother," George said to Odin, shaking his head. "I'll call the police."

No, George had to tell the cops a few times, he didn't live at the house, he had just followed Pavel from the Jewel parking lot to Odin's because he saw the guy circling, no reason for being there anymore, and thought he might be out for Odin's hide; he knew the guy was dangerous, he insisted to the police.

Knew it. Then, George said, he saw all the lights on and the back door ajar, and seeing as he was coming over to visit Odin anyway, he thought he'd come in and check if everything was okay. And then, too, he heard Odin yell, George added quickly, looking at Odin, and that made him come right in. He was glad to be useful, George said, finishing up.

Odin nodded vigorously through all of George's testimony to the police. He listened as each officer repeatedly questioned his friend, lingering on the particulars of George's job, address, surname. "Za-pa-ta," George would say slowly to each cop. Ya, sure, Odin interjected several times, the guy saved my life probably.

Pavel came out in handcuffs while all the neighbors watched bundled in their coats over bathrobes, women's hair in curlers. Mr. and Mrs. Montoya stood on their front walk and looked from the police car to Odin, to George, and back again. On their way inside, they stopped and patted Odin's shoulders; Mrs. Montoya took Odin's hand and squeezed it. Then they both looked mournfully at George and walked up their front steps.

The police dismissed George back into the house while Odin finished up with the report. They'd both have to go down to the precinct in the morning, but that, the officer said, sticking his flashlight back into his belt, was just routine. Not to worry. They'd seen Pavel's crazy state for themselves. And then everyone left, the police car silent but with its light flashing, the neighbors trotting back to their warm homes.

Odin trudged up the front stairs and into the vestibule. Someone had turned out all the lights in the living room and dining room and left just a yellow glow from the hallway and the kitchen. Odin heard clattering, running water. "George?" he called.

"Odin," George said from the kitchen, "call your sisters."

Without hesitating, Odin picked up the receiver and dialed Sonja.

While they talked, or rather while Sonja exclaimed and cried and got Harlow on the extension, Odin watched George, a dishtowel on his shoulder, as he moved from the stove, framed in the kitchen doorway, over to the sink, bringing dirty pans to be washed and then returning to the stove with the sponge to clean the surface. Odin nodded and listened to his sister and her husband. He felt like he was floating a few inches above the wool pile, the victim of some spell, like on one of those nutty TV shows.

"You gotta get out of that house," Harlow said to Odin. "That neighborhood!"

"All those crazies," Sonja said, sighing.

George came into the living room, shuffling his stockinged feet on the carpet. He smiled and winked at Odin as he picked up an empty beer glass from the coffee table and went back to the kitchen.

"Sheesh," Odin said into the phone, laughing and blushing. He turned and peeked out the drapes at the empty park.

"Are you all right?" Sonja asked.

After Odin hung up he stood listening. Nothing. The kitchen light was out. But there was still a yellow glow from the hallway.

"Hello?" Odin called. He made his way toward the light.

George was in Odin's bedroom pulling down the bedspread, the lamp on the nightstand turned down low. He had taken off his shirt and undershirt. Muscled, efficient shoulders and dark freckles on his breastbone. He still wore his watch.

Odin gripped the doorframe with one hand. "George," he said. "Oh, man."

George just smiled and neatly folded the bedspread at the bottom of the bed. Then he yanked the blanket and top sheet up and back, exposing the perfect white rectangle of bed. To Odin it was as if the earth had burst open beneath him and brought forth a newly minted, gleaming city.

Odin heard a rushing sound. "You're my first man," he said to George. In love, he meant, in the heart.

"First man and last, Odin," George said as Odin embraced him. "First and last."

UNIVERSITY PRESS OF NEW ENGLAND

publishes books under its own imprint and is the publisher for Brandeis University Press, Dartmouth College, Middlebury College Press, University of New Hampshire, Tufts University, and Wesleyan University Press.

Library of Congress Cataloging-in-Publication Data

Doenges, Judy, 1959–
What she left me : stories and novella / Judy Doenges.
p. cm.
"The Katharine Bakeless Nason literary publication prizes"
Contents: What she left me — MIB — Crooks — Solved — The money stays, the people go — Occidental — Disaster — The whole numbers of families — Incognito — God of gods.
ISBN 0–87451–937–3 (cloth : alk. paper)
 1. United States—Social life and customs—20th century—Fiction.
I. Title.
PS3554.O346W43   1999
813'.54—dc21   99-30945